More praise for
MURDER OBSERVED

"Clara is a delightful heroine. She has the values of an older generation but is tolerant of the younger one. The story moves rapidly. . . . We hope she'll be back again soon. She's a delight for those who like their murder and mystery stories well-written and without vulgarity."
The Chattanooga Times

"Ingeniously plotted . . . One of many pleasures of reading about Clara Gamadge is the combination of spunk and sweetness which characterizes her, her family and many of her friends—lively, well-read, witty, energetic people. . . . A delight to read, an even stronger mystery than her first book—a matter for rejoicing."
The Drood Review of Mystery

"Lively complications, all anchored in a well-constructed Christie plot. Generational foibles, as well as familial eccentricities, are handled with warmth and charm. Lovely proof—again—that Boylan has inherited the family writing genre."
The Kirkus Reviews

"Clara Gamadge is a detective in the honorable tradition of Hercule Poirot. . . . Boylan's writing is crisp and intelligent, her heroine endearing."
Publishers Weekly

Also by Eleanor Boylan
Published by Ivy Books:

WORKING MURDER

MURDER OBSERVED

Eleanor Boylan

1990
151 p.

IVY BOOKS • NEW YORK

Ivy Books
Published by Ballantine Books
Copyright © 1990 by Eleanor Boylan

Library of Congress Catalog Card Number: 89-28047

ISBN 0-8041-0812-9

This edition published by arrangement with Henry Holt and Company, Inc.

Manufactured in the United States of America

First Ballantine Books Edition: February 1993
Second Printing: June 1993

1

"FOUR SPADES," SAID ANNA PITMAN, "AND SHE'S young enough to be his granddaughter."

I said: "By."

Eve Ryder said: "By. Is she attractive?"

Sara Orne said: "Are we playing bridge or discussing your ex-husband's love life?" She put down a good dummy and Anna looked cheered; a good dummy could cheer Anna out of the most Stygian gloom.

She said: "Sorry. I'll shut up. She's not only attractive, she's damn beautiful. Isn't she, Clara?"

I nodded and we played in silence for a few minutes. The May rain beat on my living room windows, and the traffic on East Sixty-third Street ground slower and horns grew louder. New York City was awash.

The women at my bridge table were as familiar as family, *were* family of sorts, going back to the days of gym bloomers, upper berths, and crushes on Ronald Colman. We were all widows, Anna the most recent. Before her marriage, she had been for almost twenty years a bitter divorcée who had never forgiven her first husband for ceasing to love her.

She said now, sweeping to a small slam: "It's a classic case of 'no fool like an old fool.' Clara will tell you."

"Clara will tell you," I stood up, "that you'll never get cabs in this downpour and Port Authority will be a zoo. We'd better quit. Anybody want a drink?"

Anna did and I did and Sara and Eve went into my bedroom for their coats. Both lived in New Jersey and sensibly never drove their cars into Manhattan. Anna and I, residents here, were resigned nonowners of one.

Now Anna, probably sensing my irritation, made a great thing of collapsing the card table and straightening up.

"Leave it," I said, handing her a scotch.

"You're mad at me."

"You should be mad at yourself." I sat down and looked at her, still a slender, handsome woman in a good beige suit, hair coaxed to a good beige color.

I said: "No fool like an old fool? Forgive me, Anna, but you're a case in point. So am I for letting you drag me into this."

"She's a scheming witch."

"I liked her."

"She knows Barry has money."

I shrugged.

"Damn it, Clara, if it was your husband—"

"Or if it was yours! But it isn't. Barry hasn't been your husband in years. When will you let that man be?"

I was instantly sorry. Anna turned white and the hand that held her drink twitched, spilling half of it down her front. I got up feeling contrite and daubed at her with a paper napkin.

"Don't bother." She pushed my hand angrily away. "And forget I ever told you anything or asked for anything."

I was used to Anna's rages—all her friends were. In school they'd been tantrums. But I was unprepared for a woman of seventy to storm out of my house like a spoiled child. She pushed between Sara and Eve as they emerged from the bedroom, grabbed her fur coat, yanked open the door of my little elevator, and it shuddered down with her.

"What on earth . . . ?" Eve's sweet, pudding face was dismayed.

Shrugging out of her coat Sara said: "Okay, Clara, what brought this on? Start with the girl who's young enough to be Barry's granddaughter."

2

I walked to the window feeling remorseful. The rain was heavier than ever. "I should have kept my mouth shut. She'll get drenched out there. We don't all have canopies and door-men the way she does. Oh, Lord, look at her!"

Anna was splashing up and down waving at everything as if there were an empty cab between here and the East River.

I said: "I'm going down and get her."

"You are not." Sara pushed me into a chair and pinned me there with one of the long thin arms that had made her such a great basketball guard. "Let her stew. This is vintage Anna, you know that. She'll pile back up when she's wet enough. And I'll call Timmy. He just got his license and he'll adore coming to rescue us."

Eve and I exchanged glances. We knew this grandson of Sara's; rescue by a wild boar might be preferable. But Eve smiled like the good sport she was and dropped her coat beside Sara's.

"Sal's right. She'll be back."

"Demanding your hair dryer," said Sara, "and a hot toddy. What's eating her, Clara?"

I picked up my drink. "All right. But as soon as I tell you I'm going down there." We sat down and I realized this was going to sound as absurd as everything relating to poor Anna and Barry Lockwood, the nice man she had once been married to.

"Barry has decided to write a book about his grandfather and he's looking for a publisher. It seems Grandpa distinguished himself at the battle of Vicksburg."

They looked at me blankly.

"In the cavalry."

They continued to look at me blankly.

"The Civil War. You recall it?"

"Oh, brother." Sara closed her eyes.

"About a week ago he called me to ask for the name of Henry's publisher. He said that since Henry Gamadge's name was still respected as a writer and a scholar, perhaps as Hen-

3

ry's widow I could put in a good word for the account of Grandpa's glorious charge."

Sara groaned and Eve said: "Barry is really a dear guy. I always liked him. Didn't he retire from the army himself at some quite high rank?"

"Yes, colonel," I said, "and he *is* a dear guy." I got up and snapped on another light in the fast darkening room. "I didn't want to hurt his feelings, but I must admit my heart sank."

"I'll bet it did." Sara took a cigarette from her pocketbook and Eve snatched it and threw it into the fireplace. Sara shrugged.

I went on: "I said I didn't think Henry's publishers were in the market for family reminiscences and why didn't Barry do what a lot of people do"—I was backing toward the window—"have his book run off on a good copier and distribute it to members of the family who were always glad— Thank God! She got a cab!"

Anna was gone. My relief was immense as I came back to my chair.

Sara said: "Barry probably took a dim view of a mere copier for the sacred annals."

"Yes, he sounded a little huffy and said he thought they deserved what he called 'real publication.' I started to say that Gramps's life might be a speck hard to place, when Barry himself came up with an idea I'd hesitated to suggest: he asked what I thought of a subsidy publisher."

"What's that?" asked Eve.

"A vanity press," said Sara. "Grandpas at Vicksburg are their specialty."

"You pay them to publish your book," I said.

Eve, the dear innocent, said: "What's so bad about that? Betty McBride paid to have her cookbook published. It's called *In Betty's Kitchen*. She gave me a copy."

"Me too," said Sara.

"Me too," I said. "Well, I told Barry I thought that was a great idea. A few days later Anna called me to say that

4

Barry was writing a book about his grandfather and had gotten in touch with her regarding some albums of family photographs which he couldn't find and had they gotten in with her stuff when they split up. They had—I'm sure Anna deliberately kept them—and she was only too glad of an excuse to go up to his house in Connecticut and give them to him. She found him sitting talking to a beautiful girl from a subsidy house called Byways Press and immediately went into a jealous snit. Poor Anna.''

We were silent, all thinking, no doubt, of the systematic way in which Anna had, over the years, destroyed her husband's regard, the rivals she'd imagined—perhaps even created—the military posts across the world from which she'd fled in rage and returned in remorse, and finally the precipitous and promptly regretted divorce.

Sara said, rather bitterly: ''It isn't as if she didn't have a perfectly nice husband after that. Glenn Pitman was okay.''

Eve said, rather wistfully: ''And he left her well off.''

I said, rather callously: ''And he was lucky to die before he could suffer Barry's fate. Although . . .'' I looked at the streaming window. ''I can't imagine Anna being jealous of Glenn. It was only Barry.''

''Only and forever Barry,'' said Eve.

''Forever and ever Barry.'' Sara got up and walked to the window, taking another cigarette from her pocketbook and glaring defiantly back at Eve. ''So when did you get to meet the siren from Byways Press, Clara?''

''Anna invited her to lunch under the pretext of having some material about Barry's family, and I was asked to come and size her up. The girl's name is Elisabeth—she calls herself Beth—and she's German and gorgeous. Early twenties. She's enrolled at Columbia in a summer graduate program in journalism and she has a room in student quarters somewhere up on Morningside Drive. Byways Press—I get the impression it's kind of a dinky outfit—has an office near there. Beth told me she'd offered them her services free

in order to—as she put it—'improve her English skills.'
think her English is pretty darn good, but she's hot to im
prove it.''

"Brains, beauty, and youth," murmured Sara.

The three of us, with no great amount of those first tw
assets and none of the third, sat in depressed silence. The
I went on: "Anyway, Anna spent the whole lunch telling
Beth that despite their divorce she and Barry were 'still close
and she'd be happy to sit in on any consultations. Then Beth'
boyfriend showed up, and he's Austrian and equally gor
geous. The pair of them with their blond hair look like Sig
mund and Sieglinde.''

"Who are they? Never mind—go on." Sara stood at the
window smoking.

"The boyfriend's name is Dollfuss."

"What?"

"That's what I said. It seems he's named for his grand
father's hero, the chancellor of Austria back in the nineteer
thirties.''

"Sure." Sara snapped her fingers. "Hitler had him mur
dered. Dollfuss was a big hero-martyr to the Austrians. M
God—she's back!''

Sara was staring down into the street. We joined her, an
I could hardly believe it. Anna had materialized on the side
walk again, signaling futilely, fur coat hanging on her like
wet animal.

Eve said: "She must have been standing up against the
building to try and stay dry."

"That does it," I said. "I'm going down and get her."

I summoned my elevator, wanting to laugh, wanting t
cry. Anna! Why did I remain fond of her? But I did. A
especially devoted friend, fiercely loyal, wonderfully gen
erous, she had often exhausted my patience but never my
affection.

The downstairs hall was black as night. I switched o
the light as I left the elevator and walked past the close
door of Henry Gamadge's laboratory, thinking, as I di

6

every time, never more . . . I opened the front door and banged on the glass of the storm. I might as well have breathed on it for all I could be heard. I opened it a foot, received a faceful of rain, and yelled: "Anna! Get back in here this minute!"

She turned, then came sloshing back into the hall, bringing a torrent with her. She said: "And another thing. That—what's his name?—Dollfuss—of all the awful monikers—I can show you something that makes me think he's not on the level."

Typical. Anger forgotten. One-track mind working smoothly.

I said: "Will you kindly get back up—"

"Look at this." She pulled from the pocket of her coat's satin lining a long, ecru envelope, fattish, with several foreign stamps. The address, in a scrawled handwriting, was smeared, and the thing was limp and damp.

"What is it?" I felt my impatience returning.

"Something he didn't want me to see. When I got to Byways Press this morning—"

"Don't tell me you were there again, horning in."

"—and what a dump *that* place is—I should think Barry could have found better—and I wasn't 'horning in,' I was contributing some things from my scrapbook—well, when I got there Dollfuss was waiting for Beth and reading this." Anna shoved it back inside her pocket. "He slid it under a pile of stuff pretty quick but not before I saw the stamp and I said, 'Isn't that a German stamp? Do you have friends in Germany?' and he said—"

"Anna, will you shut up and march yourself—"

"—Oh, no, he was Austrian and he didn't know a single person in Germany. Then why was somebody in Germany writing him what looked like five or six typewritten pages? And why the dramatic denial? So I stole it."

I looked at her, aghast.

"I grabbed it when he went out to help Barry park his car. They came back with Beth and I said I had to go because I

7

had this lunch and bridge date at your place. I was going to read it in the cab but Beth offered to drive me here so I haven't had a chance to look at it, but when I get home—"

"Do you realize it's a crime to steal mail?"

"It isn't a crime to pick up a letter by mistake and then apologize and return it. Suppose this Dollfuss person has a record or something. I'm only doing it for Barry's sake. God, I'm cold." Anna shivered. "I guess you're right, I should go back up— Clara!" She stared through the streaming glass of the door. "There he is!"

"There who is?" I tried to follow her gaze.

"Dollfuss! I recognize that big old red Buick he drives." She pushed the door open, drenching me. "He's looking for a number—he's come to pick me up!"

"More likely come to pick his letter up," I said grimly.

"What letter?" Anna grinned at me through her ruined makeup, and I couldn't help laughing. I said:

"Well, close the door till the light changes and he gets here." Through the downpour I'd recognized, a few car lengths up, a handsome young face topped by yellow hair, craning out of a car window, scanning housefronts.

"Barry sent him," said Anna serenely. "Barry knew it would be hard to get a cab in this weather. How absolutely dear and wonderful of Barry."

Barry, Barry, Barry. Utterly bedraggled, Anna looked a hundred but happy. I kissed her and pushed her sopping hair back and said: "I hope you haven't caught pneumonia. The minute you're home get in a hot tub and have a nice, big—"

"I'll call you, Clara."

The traffic moved and she was out the door, was on the sidewalk, was hurrying around the front of the big red car to reach the passenger seat, was down as the car lunged forward in a seemingly helpless skid, was under, and was dead.

The sounds were screams and sirens.

The sights were horrified faces in a wet, converging crowd and the blond young driver leaping out to pry his fender from a taxi to release the blood and mink mess beneath.

8

The sensations were of Sara's and Eve's arms around me and the rain continuing to fall in the manner of a person weeping uncontrollably.

2

MY ALARM CLOCK IS OLD AND UGLY, ALSO
cheap—it cost five dollars twenty years ago—and it makes a
sound like a demented buzz saw.

I sat up in bed feeling old and ugly, and if there had been
anyone in the house to speak to I'd have sounded like a buzz
saw; but there was no one, and I got myself into the kitchen
to make coffee. My son Henry and his wife Tina would be
here in an hour to go with me to Anna's service. They lived
in Brooklyn Heights, practiced law in the same firm, and had
been kind enough to take the day off for my sake.

My utter depression of the past two days was unabated. I
looked out of the kitchen window at the budding acacia tree
in my small yard, and for the first time in its brave old life it
failed to give me pleasure. The morning sounds of traffic on
Sixty-third Street, which I usually found companionable, now
had an odious association.

The phone rang and I took the receiver from the wall and
said hello.

"Clara Gamadge, are you out of your elderly mind?"

"Sadd!"

The one person on earth who could scold me and console me simultaneously, my venerable cousin and dear
friend, Charles Saddlier, retired publisher, stubborn widower, curmudgeon extraordinary, militant convert to the
state of Florida, and known to all who had ever known
him as "Sadd."

He now went on with his customary restraint and delicacy:
"Really, Clara, you must be in your dotage. Henry phoned

me to say you've conceived an 'idée fixe' on some old school chum whom you believe to have been deliberately run over and killed.''

"She was, Sadd, she was!'' I began to blubber. "Anna said to me just *seconds* before she—''

"Wait.'' I knew he was transferring the receiver to what he fondly called his "good ear.'' "Are we talking about Anna Lockwood, wife of that noble military man Barry—''

"She divorced Barry years ago,'' I said impatiently. "She married Glenn Pitman when—''

"I don't care who she married. Nobody would want to kill Anna unless it was open season on bores.''

"Sadd, listen to me.'' I poured coffee with my free hand. "But before I say another word, thanks for this call. Long distance isn't cheap at this hour. How's Florida?''

"Florida is glorious in May, as you'd know if you'd just clear out of that preposterous city and move down. All right. So somebody murdered Anna—absurd thought of the week— but fill me in.''

I did so, gratefully, purgatively, everything from the conversation at the bridge table and its unhappy conclusion, to the swiped letter, to the last ghastly minutes on the street. I ended: "And the letter was gone.''

"Of course it was. Just stuck in her pocket like that? And the awful conditions of the weather and the accident? That letter is lying sodden at the bottom of the nearest drain to you on Sixty-third Street.''

I said nothing, and he went on: "Have you told your other two bridge-playing friends what you believe?''

"No.''

"Just Henry and Tina?''

"Yes.''

"And the police have cleared the young man?''

"Completely. It was an 'unavoidable accident' and nobody is pressing charges. Glenn's money all goes to his daughter, and Anna's to Beaver Hill—she was a devoted alumna—she has no family so you see—''

11

"You realize you may be doing this young foreigner a frightful injustice?"

I looked at the clock. "You were a dear to call, Sadd. I'm not going to let you run up a big bill, and I have to dress. When will I see you again?"

"I may get to Anna's service."

"Hardly. That's in a few hours."

"I repeat."

I froze in the act of taking the receiver from my ear.

"Sadd!"

As the three of them walked through my door an hour later I felt almost lighthearted. Sadd's smile under a crisp white mustache, new since I'd last seen him, shone on me complacently. Tina, my petite, pretty daughter-in-law, who was thirty-odd—I never could remember her exact age because she looked twenty-odd—wore a crimson suede suit which delightfully set off her short, shiny black hair. I often looked at Tina's feathery topknot and groaned at the long white mane I wore coiled on top of my head at the long since request of my husband and now of my children.

I said: "Fabulous new suit, Tina."

"What about mine?" said my son.

"Your what?"

"Suit."

"It can't be new."

"Sure it is."

Henry Gamadge Junior, like his father, was incapable of looking pressed. As I took their coats, he said: "Was I not wonderful to think of inviting Sadd up?"

"Was I not wonderful to come?" Sadd kissed me. "Actually, I have a duty visit to pay on Kathy and my appallingly spoiled grandchildren in Toronto. Might as well make a stop here. Besides, as I said to Henry, your mother can't be allowed to have one of her cuckoo-cuckoo seizures without me." He looked in the mirror over the mantel, then at me. "How do you like my mustache, Clara?"

"Love it. Very sexy."

"That's what a fifteen-year-old neighbor said. Both ends of the spectrum approving, I'll keep it."

Tina said: "Do we have time for coffee?"

"No, but we do for a Bloody Mary," said Sadd and headed for the kitchen.

I piled their coats on the sofa and then kissed my son, who had sat down in a chair over the back of which he used to climb to reach his father's shoulders.

I said: "I can't tell you what this means to me, dear. For you and Tina to take a whole day . . ."

He touched my hand. "Glad to do it, Mom. And Sadd's right—you can't be allowed to have one of your 'seizures' without us."

Tina, standing at the window, said: "It was from here that Sara and Eve saw it happen?"

"Sara did." I joined her. "Eve was in the bathroom."

"Bird's-eye view of tragedy." Tina took my arm. "I'm afraid it'll be a while before you can look out of this window without feeling awful."

From his chair Henry said: "Sara didn't see what you— you think you saw?"

"She said she saw the car skid."

"Of course she did." Sadd emerged from the kitchen with a tray. "Because that's all there was to see. Now then— Bloody Mary for me, same for Clara. Henry's driving, so leftover coffee for him and Tina." He put the tray on the coffee table and came to the window. "Clara, why can't you just go along with what Sara saw?"

"Because I saw his wheels and I saw his face and I know he took the letter."

Nobody said whose wheels or which face or what letter because I'd been weeping and fuming about those wheels and that face and that letter for two days.

Sadd said: "So he looked scared. You'd look scared too if you were skidding."

"He wasn't scared. And he wasn't skidding. He was gunning."

They looked at me with a kind of patient horror.

Henry said: "Poor neurotic Anna makes a remark about his not being 'on the level' and shows you a piece of mail that could have been from his mother. That's all you have to go on?"

"That and his face."

"That face!" Sadd rolled his eyes. "It's beginning to take shape in my mind as the face of a fiend."

"Actually, he's very handsome," I said.

They'd stopped looking at me and were looking at each other. I took a sip of my Bloody Mary and realized it would be a mistake to finish it. I put it on the mantel and took my coat from a chair. My depression had returned, and with it nervousness as I felt a paper protruding from the coat pocket. I pulled it out and said: "I want to read you this. Tell me if it sounds corny."

"What is it?" Tina moved from the window.

I swallowed. "Barry asked me to write what he called 'a few words of tribute.' I'm to read it when Anna's ashes are spread."

Sadd said: "For God's sake, why you?"

"I guess there's no one else." My nervousness was turning into embarrassment. "Anna had no children, no living relatives, her stepdaughter may or may not be there, and her ex-husband can hardly do it. I think it was kind of him to think of it at all." I stuffed the thing back in the pocket and ended miserably: "I guess I was her closest friend."

Henry stood up. "Read it to us in the car. We'd better roll if we're going to make Connecticut by noon."

Getting out of Manhattan on that weekday mid-morning was the usual exasperating struggle. We crept and inched and crawled and stalled and Sadd kept asking what he was doing here and Henry swore. In the backseat Tina and I discussed little Henry's progress in the second grade, but none of us seemed to want to talk much at all, and we rode mostly in silence till we emerged with a general sigh of relief onto the Saw Mill River Parkway. Now progress became

14

possible, even pleasant, with the pale green of spring materializing everywhere.

Tina pulled Anna's "tribute" from my pocket and said: "Read this to us."

"You'll probably think it's awful," I said, "and reading in a car makes me sick."

Henry said: "Quit stalling, Mom. Tina, you read it."

"No, I will." I took my glasses from my pocketbook and read rapidly and carelessly what I'd composed slowly and painstakingly the night before.

"Friendships that are made in youth and last a lifetime are bound to be special ones. My friendship with Anna dates from a September day in 1931 when we were both lonely new arrivals at boarding school. Generosity and loyalty were qualities that she was to display all her life toward her friends. Those of us who remember these qualities will miss her."

I cleared my throat. "It's the best I could do. How does it sound?"

"Like Zamfir and his panflute," said Sadd.

"I know it's sentimental but I couldn't seem to—"

"It's fine, Clara." Tina took the paper from me and stuffed it back in my pocket. "Read it just the way it is."

Henry said kindly: "I think it's a masterpiece of tact and brevity."

"Thank you, dear."

Sadd said: " 'Was to display' is awkward. You don't need the future perfect. Just the past tense 'displayed' would be—"

"I didn't ask you to edit it," I said crossly. Sadd was a dedicated grammarian; you didn't safely stay in the wrong tense with Sadd around.

The bordering green intensified as we sped along the parkway and I began to look for my favorite sign of spring, the lovely, mustardy smudge of willows. Signs for the Taconic

15

Parkway began to appear and Henry said: "Break out the Colonel's directions. I'd guess we're taking the Taconic."

I rooted in my pocketbook again and produced a typed paragraph with a map in red ink. I said: "We can thank Barry for his military precision. This map looks like a field general's. You read, Tina."

It was true that reading in a car made me queasy, and in this case queasiness was enhanced by dread of the coming ordeal.

Tina read: "Directions to the town of Lake Winifred, Connecticut: take the Taconic Parkway to Route 44 east, then thirty miles to Route 41 north. Two miles up, a small lake for which the town is named will appear on your right. Turn left at this corner and The Chapel in the Elms, a small, non-denominational church, is a quarter-mile on the right. Anna's service will be held here at noon. Directly behind the chapel is my cottage, where I hope you will all come to lunch. Allow about three hours from Manhattan. Lake Winifred is in the southern Berkshires, halfway between ritzy Sharon, Connecticut and rural Sheffield, Massachusetts. We are more rural than ritzy."

Sadd chuckled. "Barry has a nice feel for alliteration."

"Do you know him, Sadd?" Tina handed the directions over the seat to Henry.

"Slightly. I think I first met him at your wedding, Clara."

"You did. You and Harriet sat at the table with Barry and Anna and Aunt Robby."

"Good God, what a memory." Sadd stared back at me. "I recall now that Barry was in uniform. It was shortly before we all were. A friend of mine had been in his class at West Point. By the way, did you say he's writing his military memoirs or something?"

"A life of his grandfather. He's given it to a vanity press. That's how he met Beth."

Henry grinned at me in the rearview mirror. "Is she the young lovely he's taken up with?"

I said, feeling irritated: "She's young and she's lovely but I'm not sure he's 'taken up with her' in the sense you mean."

"Why shouldn't he?" asked Sadd. "I'm jealous as hell."

Tina said: "You may not be the only jealous one. If that Austrian boyfriend of hers finds out, Barry better be on guard for that big old red Buick. Oops—sorry, Clara. That was tactless."

She'd seen me wince and grabbed my hand contritely.

I said: "I dreamed about that big old red Buick last night. It was bearing down on my bed. How much farther, Henry?"

"We should be there in about half an hour."

We rode in silence for a while, then Henry cleared his throat in the elaborate way his father used to when he was about to broach a sensitive subject. He said: "I have a question, Mom. You said Anna and Barry were divorced years ago after a rocky marriage. Anna remarried and lived in New Jersey till her husband died, then moved to Manhattan. How come she's being buried in Lake Winifred, Connecticut, practically in her first husband's backyard?"

I looked out of the window. "For a reason only her old friends know. The summer that they bought the Lake Winifred cottage, Anna had a baby son, born a few weeks after Barry went overseas. He never saw the child. It only lived two days and is buried in the churchyard we're going to now. Anna made Barry promise that her ashes would be spread on the child's grave."

They were silent, properly affected, I hoped, by my story. And it *was* affecting. Poor Anna had been sufficiently trashed, I felt. She'd had her share of woe, and if that wretched Dollfuss had, for whatever reason, deliberately mown her down, I was going to know why.

"Here's the turn," said Henry, slowing.

A small, weedy body of water had come into sight on our right.

Sadd murmured: "Lake Winifred is not to be confused with Lake Louise."

We made the turn and almost at once a pretty white church was visible, set back on a rise, nicely framed by elms. Henry and Sadd said something simultaneously about how charming it was, and Tina pointed elaborately to a small cemetery

17

alongside it. But they were trying to distract me from something we'd all seen.

Partially concealed by trees across the road from the church was a big old red Buick.

3

I LITERALLY CHOKED.

"He can't have the gall—the absolute gall to come here!"

"Take it easy, Mom." Henry turned into the church drive-way. "At least he didn't bring the thing in here." We pulled up beside one of four cars in the parking lot. "Isn't that your friend Sara?"

The familiar figure emerging from one of the cars re-minded me that my distress must be confined to present com-pany. I said: "Just promise you won't let him come near me."

"Pretty poor taste to come at all," said Sadd. "Which one is he?"

Henry and Sadd had gotten out of the car and now stood looking at a little group on the church steps a hundred yards away. I was simply not ready to move, and Tina stayed with me.

Sara opened the door beside me and clambered in. "Did you see what I saw?"

"Sal, I don't think you've met Henry's wife, Tina."

"Hi, Tina, my God, I'm sure he thought he tucked that car out of sight, but could you miss it if you'd seen it the way we—"

"You know what I think?" Tina was gazing out of the car window at the group on the church steps. "I think he isn't here."

Sara and I stared past her. Barry Lockwood's tall figure dominated the group and there were five others: a stout, middle-aged woman in a bright blue suit, a balding man, Beth, Eve, and a short clergyman in some indefinable vestment.

Sara said: "Then what the hell is that car doing here?"

Henry turned and said: "All set, girls? Let's join the party."

We got out. I introduced Sara to Sadd. Then she and Henry tried to recall the last time they'd met, and Sara told Henry he looked more like his father than ever. My eyes were upon Barry, who detached himself from the group and was hurrying toward us. I watched the approaching figure with iron-gray hair, weathered face, and only slightly stooping shoulders, remembering when the first was fair, the second ruddy, and the third erect. Like most military men, Barry never looked quite as dashing out of uniform as in it, but his appearance was subtly appealing and his manner unfailingly pleasant.

"Clara, bless you." He kissed me. "Sadd, this is too good to be true. Sara, you were great to come. And this has to be another Henry Gamadge."

By the time he got to Tina and Henry had introduced her, a second figure had started toward us. Beth—I couldn't for the life of me think of her last name—with her long, light hair and yellow coat, looked rather like a wood nymph emerging from leafy surroundings. She touched Barry's arm and he turned with a look that, I must admit, could only be described as fatuous.

She said, in her very good English and slight, charming accent: "Colonel, may I explain about the car?"

"Of course, Beth. Friends, this is Beth Bauer."

"You see—and oh, I am so sorry—you see, the car is mine. Dollfuss was only driving it that—that day . . ." She spoke hurriedly, her distress evident. "I wish I would not have brought it, but I had no other way to get here. Without it I could not have come. I thought I had placed it far enough back so it would be not visible, but Mrs. Ryder saw it and it upset her and perhaps upset you too?"

I nodded and the girl went on disjointedly: "Oh, I am so sorry—I plan to sell it—I cannot bear to drive it—oh, you nuzz forgive me—please, you muzz!"

Her rare slip in pronunciation, undoubtedly caused by agitation, was unexpected and a little touching.

"Beth," said Barry gently, his arm around her, "we understand."

We didn't—at least, I didn't—but whatever you say, Barry.

"Now," he went on, "let me introduce you to these folks. You know Mrs. Gamadge . . ."

I studied the girl. She looked at me imploringly between each introduction. Was I being dense? Missing a message? Was her distress only because of the car? Surely she could have rented one. She said: "Just one more thing: Dollfuss asked me to tell you how deeply, deeply sorry he is and that he will never forgive himself—"

"For what?" Sadd moved briskly to Beth's side. "For an unavoidable accident? Barry, if you'll allow me, I'll spend the rest of the day trying to reassure this lovely creature."

We all laughed and Beth looked relieved.

Barry said: "Before you start your reassuring act, Sadd, we'd better join the others."

We started to drift toward the chapel and I said: "Beth, this has been awful for you in a special way."

"I have hardly slept since it happened."

"Well, you'll sleep tonight." Barry's arm was still around her. "I'm going to insist that you stay next door with a friend of mine, and she'll see to it that you sleep."

Beth said to everyone: "Colonel Lockwood has been wonderful to me. We're working on the life of his grandfather. It's going to be wonderful."

Oh, sure, wunnerful, wunnerful. We'd reached the other group and there were more introductions; I felt as if everyone present had been introduced ten times. The balding man and the woman in the blue suit turned out to be Mr. and Mrs. Hazen, Anna's stepdaughter and husband, whom I'd heard Anna mention but had never met. Eve huddled between Sara

and me, whispering that she wished she hadn't come. I wa
conscious of a slight chill in the breeze.

Now the clergyman, adorned in what appeared to be
giant stole of quilted, flowered cotton, addressed us: "My
friends, our departed sister Anna has requested that her ashe
be spread on the grave of her infant son. If you will follow
me into the chapel where the ashes now repose, we wil
pause there to ask God's blessing upon our sister and upon
those gathered here, for we are all mortal and this is a salu
tary time to reflect on it. Then we will proceed out the side
door of the chapel to the place where Mrs. Gamadge, a dea
friend of the deceased, will speak a few words and perform
our little rite."

There was a sharp intake of breath at my shoulder and
was pretty sure Sadd had winced at the last words.

"Shush," I whispered.

"I don't object to 'rite.' It is one. But doesn't he realiz
that 'our' and 'little' diminish the—"

"Shut *up*."

We were entering the chapel, and I hoped this mutteree
exchange had not reached the ears of Mr. and Mrs. Hazen
who were beside me. But her eyes were as vacant as when
she'd said how do you do, and he was looking at his watch.

The interior of the chapel was cheerful and nondescript
with clear windows and light brown pews. We trailed down
the aisle and came to a halt before a raised table from which
the bestoled reverend took a black enameled box and then
asked us to bow our heads.

He began to make his speech and I began to rehearse
mine. Should I read it? Plow through it from memory?
could barely recall a full sentence of it now, and only the
offending future perfect came readily to mind. When woul
this ordeal be over? We were being reminded that time pass
eth all too swiftly, and a sigh from Sadd echoed my own
feelings that it was fine with me; in fact, on this occasio
time could even pick up its pace a bit.

I felt a nudge from Tina and realized that the enamelee

box was being extended to me. I took it and we filed out to a shaded portico and a beautiful little churchyard. A single big elm shaded most of it, and there were flower beds and many old graves and some new ones. But what had happened to the weather? The sun was gone and there were scattered drops of rain. We were led to a corner where, under a bursting forsythia bush, there was a little headstone.

I hadn't expected to be overwhelmed and neither, I'm sure, had anyone else, but I knew from the motionless figures around me that they were as paralyzed as I by the sheer poignancy of the moment. We stood in absolute silence till I began to dimly suppose that I was on. I dragged my eyes to the face of the clergyman and he nodded encouragingly.

I opened the box and took a few steps forward. They must have been faltering ones because Henry was beside me at once and his arm was around me.

My son's touch unlocked me. I said: "Anna, dear, we hope your spirit is with your son's and with God."

I emptied the ashes beside the stone, thrust the box at Henry, and made for a wooden bench a few yards away. It was years since I'd quit, but I'd have given a hundred dollars for a cigarette.

Sara and Eve hurried toward me and Tina and Beth followed. Mrs. Hazen and the men remained standing where they were, and Mr. Hazen checked his watch again.

Barry called: "My house. That path through the hedge."

The back porch of a yellow cottage was visible across the lawn, but I knew I had to have a couple of minutes to collect myself.

I said: "I saw a Ladies' at the back of the church. Please, all of you go ahead to Barry's and I'll—"

"We'll wait for you," said Sara and Eve together.

"Please go—*please*."

I must have sounded as urgent as I felt, for no one followed me as I hurried down the path and back into the chapel. The spotless little rest room had a sofa, and I sat on it and wept for a while. I wished desperately that I could go home. I

23

wanted to do just two things—talk to Barry alone, and confront a certain young murderer—and I saw scant possibility of either.

Finally I got up and stood in front of the mirror, pulled the hairpins from my hair and wondered why I had worn this suit. It made me look fat; but not as fat as Mrs. Hazen, I thought meanly. I twisted what my grandson calls my horse's tail up into a fresh knot on top of my head and jabbed hairpins into it. Two pretty cloisonné combs my daughter had given me took care of the back, and I stared at myself, decided I looked awful, and walked back into the church.

Barry was sitting in the back pew. He stood up, held out his hand, and drew me in beside him.

"Clara, thank you."

"Oh, Barry, for what?"

"For what you said."

"I don't even know what I said."

"It was very like what the chaplain in England said when he broke the bad news to me. He said, 'You will know this child someday.' I didn't believe it, but I guess he did, and it was rather consoling at the time. Now, I have some *good* news, and I want you to be the first to know."

"Lovely," I said nervously, "but shouldn't we be getting back to the house? You can tell me as we—"

"No rush. My neighbor is there and she's kindly gotten everything ready. By the way, can you and Sadd stay awhile after the others have gone? I want to talk to you. I'll drive you back to New York tonight."

I said happily: "I can't answer for Sadd. He's on his way to Toronto to visit his daughter. But I'd love to."

"Good. Now for my news: I'm going to be married next week."

Oh, Lord, I thought, oh, Lord. "Oh, Barry," I said, "oh, Barry, that *is* nice news."

"We're going to tell everybody after lunch. Not a word now."

"Not a word."

24

The door of the chapel opened and Sadd put his head in. He said: "I mustn't come farther into the sacred premises because I have a drink in hand. We're waiting for you two."

4

THE SUN CAME OUT AGAIN AS THE THREE OF US walked across the lawn to Barry's house and I tried to thrust from my mind all thought of the upcoming December-May nuptials. Every fiber of me knew that the odds were against success for such a marriage, but it was none of my business and, I thought grimly, better the girl marry Barry than a murderer.

We went around to the front of the house past lilac bushes exuding perfume, and as we walked up the three steps to the front door, Barry said: "Sadd, Clara's staying awhile when the others have left. I wish you would too. I'd like your opinion on something."

"Fine with me." Sadd looked at me, his eyebrows sky high.

I said: "Barry will drive us back later. You can stay at my place."

Barry said, as he opened the front door: "It concerns the young man Beth's involved with, Dollfuss Moltke."

My heart gave a small lurch and I was grateful for the smiles and words of welcome that greeted us, for by now I was sure Sadd's eyebrows were in the stratosphere.

I said: "Barry, you've added a sun porch!"

"Yes, when I retired."

"It's lovely. What a view!"

"I knew I'd be spending most of my time here. I've always loved the Berkshires. That's the southern range. Too bad it's so misty."

An attractive, sixtyish woman turned from a buffet set

under a window and was introduced as Mrs. Doris Manning, the kind neighbor responsible for this feast. Feast indeed, I said, as she poured me a glass of wine and said she'd heard I'd earned it and I was to call her Doris. Barry was heaping a plate for me, and I glanced around, taking in the distribution of the mourning party.

Sara and Eve had sacrificed themselves on the altar of the Hazens. Mrs. Hazen was showing them pictures of her grandchildren, and her husband was wolfing his lunch. On the sun porch Henry and Tina and Beth were hitting it off, and Sadd wandered out to sit with them and stare at Beth.

Doris said these rolls were cold and there were more in the oven.

"I'll get 'em." Barry hastened toward the kitchen. Oh God, I thought, he's so happy. I drained my wineglass and asked Doris if that was her house I saw a corner of through the window.

"Yes. It amuses people when I tell them it's also the house I was born in."

"Really?" I wanted to sound interested because I was, but I was also dreading Barry's announcement and wishing there was some way to cushion it. Sara was notoriously outspoken, and I didn't for a minute trust Sadd not to blurt out something that might best remain unblurted. But I could scarcely trot around whispering to all to brace themselves.

". . . left to me when my parents died," Doris was saying, "and I raised my own family in it. My husband was postmaster here. When he died I was able to take over. I retired last year."

I looked with respect at this nice woman and wouldn't at all have minded chatting on, but Sara was bearing down on us for a refill and a respite.

"That pasta is out of this world. Clara, you're going to enjoy talking to Lillian Hazen. She has six grandchildren and many lovely pictures of each."

This in a loud voice. You see what I mean about Sara. Doris won my heart by winking at me. She piled pasta on Sara's plate, then asked her to pass the bowl around. Sara seized it and headed for the sun porch. Clearly my duty was to rescue Eve. I took a basket of steaming rolls from Barry as he emerged from the kitchen and sat down beside the Hazens.

Eve said gratefully: "Couldn't you eat those rolls forever? Clara, you must see these pictures." She transferred an alarmingly large pile from her lap to mine. Mr. Hazen reached for a roll and said: "Mrs. Gamadge would want to see those other ones, Lil."

"Oh, yes." She produced an elderly, much-creased manila envelope. "I didn't know what to do with this. I found it in a box in Anna's apartment. They asked me to go up there and clear the place out. It's a lot of pictures from before she married my dad. I think you're in some of them, Mrs. Gamadge, and the Colonel too."

She dug into the envelope and pulled out a wad of curling black and white photographs, most of them the tiny, yellow-tinged products of one's first Brownie, one or two enlargements to the vast size of perhaps five by seven, all redolent of summers in the nineteen twenties and thirties, a fragile mass of memories.

"My hubby says I should give them to you if you want them."

The room rocked. From the envelope had slid a single eight-by-ten photograph, and in it I'd caught a glimpse of the face of Dollfuss Moltke, my handsome young murderer. I was not mad, drunk, or obsessed. I'd seen his face as Lillian shuffled through the stack.

"What a kind thought," I think I said. "May I really have them?"

"Oh, sure. Maybe the Colonel would like—"

"I'll show them to him." My fingers closed greedily over the lot, and the face of Dollfuss flashed up at me again as I slid the pictures back into the envelope. The fact that not a photograph there was less than forty years old, and Dollfuss was probably twenty-five, meant nothing. I'd seen his face.

Mr. Hazen did his regular time check. "We have to get

back to Albany and I hate to drive after dark. You want to get me another piece of that pie, Lil?''

She got up and went to the buffet. I looked around. Eve had vanished. Sadd, heading toward me with a coffeepot, saw the array of pictured childlife in my lap and made a U-turn.

''Sadd,''I hailed him determinedly, ''the Hazens have to go shortly. I know you'll want to talk to them. I'll do the coffee.''

I wrested the pot from him and went out to the porch clutching the envelope. I sat down beside Tina, and Henry relieved me of the coffeepot.

Beth was saying: ''I teased him about his nickname, 'Dolly,' because it sounds funny for a boy, but it is quite a natural short way to say 'Dollfuss,' and of course 'dolly' does not have the same meaning in German as it does in English.''

Was I hearing things?

Henry said: ''Beth is telling us about her friend Dollfuss. He showed her a picture of himself with his mother and the words 'Dolly, age twelve' written on the back.''

Beth said: ''I think Mrs. Gamadge knows he is named for the chancellor of Austria who was his grandfather's hero. Do you remember the day—''

''I remember.'' I probably sounded curt, because Tina said: ''Clara's exhausted. I can tell. We should go soon.''

Sara and Eve echoed her words and stood up.

I said grimly: ''Not before the announcement.''

They looked at each other questioningly, and behind me Sadd's voice said: ''Announcement?'' The Hazens, I saw, were on their feet. The moment had come.

Beth said, with an exquisite smile: ''Yes. Colonel Lockwood has something to tell all of you.''

I could at least thank the girl for this warning of sorts. Tina and Henry and I sat mute. Sara grasped one of my shoulders and Eve the other as if for support. Sadd walked quickly into the living room and said: ''Barry, where's your bathroom?''

29

"Through the bedroom, but this will only take a second, Sadd." Barry put a restraining hand on Sadd's arm. "I have some great news: a lovely lady has promised to marry me, and we hope you'll all come to our wedding next Thursday right here in the chapel."

He put his arm around Doris's shoulder and kissed her.

Doris smiled at Sadd. "If it's a real hurry call, Mr. Saddlier, you may be the first to kiss the bride."

It was a good thing the Hazens laughed loudly and closed in on the happy couple. It was a good thing Sadd leaned somewhere in the vicinity of Doris's cheek, then vanished. It was a good thing Beth said: "Isn't it lovely? The Colonel told me yesterday," and went in to embrace the bride, for the rest of us sat or stood like dummies.

My son has a way of starting to laugh that is very like his father. It begins with an agitation of the stomach and emerges in a kind of strangled chortle that's extremely contagious. I managed to say, "On our feet!" and we went in to add our felicitations.

My happiness for Barry and the utter appropriateness of the thing made me almost giddy. Doris looked delighted, even a little astonished at our jubilation, and when Sadd returned from the bathroom and proposed a toast, she said charmingly that she herself would like to drink one to the nice new friends she'd made today. Well, hear, hear! And was there to be a wedding trip? Greece! Superb at this time of year! The merriment continued, survived the departure of the Hazens, of Sara and Eve, and muted touchingly when Barry begged Beth, as she put on her coat, to stay overnight with the bride-to-be. That lady added her plea.

Beth smiled at them both. "Thank you, but I have a dinner engagement."

There was a small, uncomfortable silence. Barry frowned and I thought of that murderous car awaiting her.

Barry said: "We'll walk you to the car."

He and Henry and Sadd departed. I longed to pounce on the manila envelope but must perforce help Doris and Tina carry dishes to the kitchen.

30

Doris said, scraping a plate: "I hope Barry isn't misjudging Beth's young man."

Tina and I looked at each other. She said "In what way?"

"I'll let him tell you. It's really none of my business. You're staying awhile, aren't you, Mrs. Gamadge?"

I said yes and please call me Clara. I told Tina of Barry's request.

"Sounds good. We should split. Hen's home from school by now and Teresita can only stay till six."

She gave Doris both her hands in the nice way Tina has and thanked her for "the 'spread,'" as my grandmother would call it." Now, about the wedding: what day was it to be? (Would I never get to that envelope?) Next Thursday at six in the evening? We would certainly all be there, and what would Doris like for a wedding present?

We'd worked our way to the back door and the three men were coming across the lawn. The sun was holding its own and there were lovely, low pinkish clouds over the Berkshires. Good-byes were said and Henry and Tina went through the hedge to their car. I turned back into the house, saying to myself *Now!*

As Barry and Sadd came through the door Barry was saying: "And if that guy Dollfuss is Austrian I'm Chinese."

5

DORIS HAD MADE FRESH COFFEE AND NOW stood beside us, pot in hand, looking down at the photograph on top of the pile I'd spilled out on the coffee table. Barry and Sadd and I had pulled chairs to it and we all stared in silence at the face that had leaped up at me from the group in the picture. Anna's handwriting across the bottom told us: "Olympic Games, Germany, 1936."

Barry said: "It's Dollfuss's grandfather. It has to be. My God, the likeness is incredible."

Doris said: "You mean, if the young man were to walk in here now—"

"The resemblance would stun you," I said.

"Some people have powerful genes," murmured Sadd.

Barry sat back in his chair. "In a minute I'll tell you why I've distrusted this Dollfuss—and I have—from the day he first appeared with Beth. But you first, Clara. You look as if you have a problem with him too. What is it?"

"I think he murdered Anna. Deliberately ran over her."

Barry sat up with a jerk and Doris gasped and set the coffeepot down. Barry looked from me to Sadd.

"Is this news to you, Sadd?"

"No. I was let in on the awful suspicion."

Barry's eyes went back to the photograph. He said slowly: "Before I ask you why, Clara, let me say this: he certainly comes from the right stock for it."

We all gazed hypnotically at the picture.

Sunlight poured into the packed stadium in Munich. How attractive Anna looked with her shoulder-length hair and floppy felt hat. Beside her Barry was hatless, his bulky wool sweater one that I actually remembered Anna knitting. In the row behind them were two young German officers, swastikas much in evidence on uniforms. One of them had the face of Dollfuss Moltke.

" 'Grandpa was a Nazi.' " Sadd savored the words. "What a great title for a memoir."

What was suddenly wrong about the name Dollfuss? I was struggling to think.

Barry leaned forward, studying the photograph. "I remember this picture so well. Anna and I had been married in May. I was stationed at Fork Devens in Massachusetts that summer and some of us went to Germany for the games. This was one of those deals where a photographer roams around taking snaps and you gave him the money and your address and he mailed it. Anna had this on her bureau for years."

We sat in silence as Barry continued to study the photo. Then he jabbed at it with his forefinger.

"I even remember turning around and talking to these two guys, asking them what branch of the army they were in. They were SS men. It had just been formed and Heinrich Himmler headed it up."

"What exactly does SS mean?" Doris asked. "I can't remember."

"Schutzstaffel," said Barry grimly. "Black Shirts."

"Hitler's elite group," said Sadd.

"His best bullyboys." Barry jabbed at the picture again. "This short, pudgy guy talked a lot about Jews. The tall one spent his time bad-mouthing Jesse Owens. Great pair."

Barry put the picture back on the coffee table and I picked it up and looked at the handsome young face so like the one that had haunted my thoughts for two days and two nights. The pudgy officer wore his military cap, but our man's was off in the act of being waved. His light hair shone in the sun.

Barry said: "Now the question is this: why did poor Anna have to be murdered?"

33

"If indeed she was," said Sadd. "Clara's reasons for thinking so are rather scant and emotional."

I glared at him and told Barry and Doris my reasons. They listened with gratifying respect, then Barry got up and started to walk about the room. He said: "Let me think what happened that day . . . I went to New York in the morning to work with Beth at the Byways office. Dollfuss was there. So was Anna." Barry put his hand to his head. "Poor Anna was always showing up with useless bits of memorabilia . . . She left when I came in, said she was going for lunch and bridge at your house, Clara, and Beth offered to drive her. When Beth got back we worked pretty much all day. At what point Dollfuss realized his letter was gone—if he did—I couldn't say. But when I saw the rain and said I thought I'd pick up Anna, he did insist—quite vehemently, now that I think of it—that he be allowed to do it. I said okay and they left."

"They?"

"He and Beth."

"She wasn't with him."

Barry considered this. "He must have dropped her off somewhere. If he was planning an 'accident' he wouldn't want her with him."

"How could he 'plan' this one?" said Sadd.

"He couldn't, of course," I said. "It had to be spur of the moment. Just an incredibly lucky break that he grabbed."

"My God, to think I provided him with it!" Barry groaned and sat down again, his head in his hands. Doris stood beside him and poured more coffee, keeping her other arm around his shoulder. Then he looked up and said: "The question still remains: why?"

Doris said, starting toward the kitchen: "Maybe he'd seen that picture and was afraid Anna would pick up on it—like we have."

I shook my head regretfully. "You don't kill a person just because she has a picture of somebody who might be your grandfather."

34

Sadd said: "You might if he *is* your grandfather and he was a Nazi and you're a Nazi too."

"May I point out"—Barry looked around at us—"that it is not a crime to belong to the Nazi party? Detestable maybe, but not criminal. Unless . . . you're involved in something subversive . . ."

I said slowly, knowing Sadd would pounce: "Then there's the matter of the letter. That could answer the 'why.' "

"That damn letter!" Sadd didn't fail me. "You have absolutely no proof that Dollfuss took it or that he even knew Anna had it. I repeat: it's lying in rotting fragments at the bottom of some Manhattan sewer."

"In any event, it's gone and can't help us." Barry stood up again. "And if Dollfuss—"

"Wait!" I found myself on my feet. The itch in my mind regarding the name Dollfuss had been scratched. "Has it occurred to anyone that Dollfuss said he was named for his *grandfather's hero*, the chancellor of Austria? One of Hitler's big enemies?" I stared down at the swastika on the waving cap. "So how could that be Grampa?"

They were silent, then Sadd said:

"Maybe it isn't."

"Maybe it is!" Barry was almost shouting. " 'Dollfuss' is a fake name! It's a clever touch to make him sound like an Austrian patriot. A fake name for a fake Austrian!"

"I hate to say this, Barry," and I did, "but Beth said she saw a childhood picture of him identifying him as 'Dolly.' "

"I don't care what she saw!" Barry was getting mad. "I've talked to this guy. He's charming and educated and when we've discussed Germany—I was stationed there for two years—he's deplored the Third Reich with the best of us. But I know his type . . . I know his type." Barry ground his fist into his hand. "You bet he isn't 'on the level,' as Anna said, and she knew it. I want Beth to know it too. She's a lovely girl and I don't want her to go on with him."

Doris had returned. She pushed Barry gently down into his chair and said: "Will you excuse me? I think I'll go along home. Don't move." Her restraining hand held Barry. "You

35

either, Mr. Saddlier.'' She smiled at him and then at me. ''I hope you'll both come to our wedding.''

Sadd assured her that he would try, and I assured her that I would come. I hope I didn't sound too abstracted. That letter . . . that letter . . . that letter . . .

Despite her protest, Barry rose and walked Doris out.

''I think you should tell them now,'' I heard her say.

Tell us what? I wondered vaguely as their footsteps faded. Sadd and I sat there, and I sipped my cold coffee, and Sadd said he didn't think Barry would mind if he made himself a drink and got up and went to the kitchen.

I called: ''Humor me. Let's fantasize for a minute.''

''Fantasize away.'' The refrigerator door slammed.

''Suppose the letter *was* incriminating.''

''In what way?''

''That's what I'm asking you. And myself . . . In what possible way? You first.''

''Well,'' Sadd's voice became indulgent, ''how's this: Dollfuss is a fugitive from justice.''

''Anna did say, 'suppose he has a record.' ''

Sadd came back with ice in a glass. ''So let's go with Anna, a creature of infinite imagination; the letter contained a blackmail threat. The correspondent will tip off the U.S. authorities unless Dollfuss forks over X amount. Anna must be prevented from doing her own tipping. No, I like this better . . .''

Sadd swirled his ice and warmed to his subject: ''Grandpa Dollfuss is one of the minor Nazi war criminals hidden away in a nursing home in Queens under an assumed name, kept there by his devoted grandson. One day, as Anna is pouring forth an avalanche of invaluable contributions to Barry's book, the fateful picture appears. Dollfuss is present and starts guiltily! Has Anna noticed it or noted the resemblance? He can't be sure. Now the letter arrives from the Young Nazi Bucks, or whatever they call themselves, detailing plans for getting Gramps out of the U.S.A. since rumor has it the Feds are on his trail. Anna snatches the letter—Gramps is revealed as a scoundrel—Dollfuss is one too—actually, I

36

should say 'one also' because 'one too' always sounds as if 'three four' should follow. Written, there isn't a problem, but spoken . . .''

Sadd continued to digress on the vagaries of the language. I stared out of the window, where the light was fading. Doris appeared briefly, then vanished up some stairs.

Sadd was saying: "I wonder where Barry keeps his liquor."

"Dry bar on the sun porch," said Barry coming through the back door. "Make me one too."

"One also," said Sadd.

"Me also," I said, and transferred from my chair to the sofa. "And before we say another word, Barry, let me tell you how happy we are for you. What a swell lady."

"Isn't she?" Barry sank down beside me.

Sadd called from the porch: "I heard Doris say you were to tell us something—that she's had five husbands, all living? Who cares?"

Barry laughed and reached for the photograph which still lay before us, nostalgic but sinister. He studied it for a few seconds, then put it down but continued to look at it.

"Poor Anna. I really loved her but she wouldn't believe it. Oh, sometimes she did, but mostly she believed I loved somebody—anybody—else. Even after she divorced me . . .'' He shook his head. "Do you know that as late as last week I believe she was actually jealous of Beth?"

We accepted drinks from Sadd, who sat down on a straight chair across the coffee table from us. The room was quite shadowy now. Barry's voice was low but distinct.

"She kept saying to me, 'Remember, Barry, that girl is young enough to be your granddaughter.' Well, not so surprising . . . She *is* my granddaughter."

6

"THERE WERE THOUSANDS OF CASES LIKE MINE in 1946," said Barry. "Thousands."

"Well, maybe hundreds," said Sadd.

We were nearing Manhattan, and with the parkways behind us, were forced, to my relief, into a more reasonable rate of speed. Barry, who'd said he didn't mind driving because it gave him something to do, had done a rather headlong descent from Connecticut. I pulled my feet up on the spacious backseat of the car and decided it was time for details. Darkness helped. The three of us looking straight ahead at the oncoming lights of the city helped. Confidences are easier when encapsulated in night and motion.

I said: "Barry, start with the girl who was—is?—Beth's grandmother."

"Is. Her name is Karla. She's in her eighties now. She lives in Germany."

Dimly seen in the dark of the car, Barry's profile was set and somber.

"I was with the occupation in Wiesbaden. Anna had done one of her usual crazy walkouts. She was sure there was somebody else, and of course there wasn't. Funny, isn't it? Anna literally drove me to that girl."

Barry was silent for a few seconds and the car picked up speed. He went on: "Karla was very sweet, a few years older than me. She'd been married to a German officer who was killed at the Bulge. She worked on the base. The Germans loved jobs on the base because it meant a hot lunch. Karla worked in the library. She used to save string."

38

Barry braked for a small car that buzzed importantly and dangerously past. His flow seeming to have stopped, Sadd said helpfully: "String?"

"Yes. It came around the bundles of magazines and books from the States. Karla said she was knitting a blanket for her mother. I remember thinking, My God, what good would a string blanket be in that weather? It was one of the worst winters on record, and the Germans were on their beam ends. So of course I went to the PX and bought a blanket and nothing would do but I had to go to their flat—god-awful, dismal place—and let her mother thank me. Beginning of the inevitable. Karla was pathetic and grateful and I was alone and depressed. Just before the baby was born I found out I was being transferred back to the States. It was a girl and Karla named her Louise."

Barry was over the speed limit by no more than five miles but his voice told me he'd be climbing.

I said, probably nervously: "I'd love a cup of coffee. Could we stop?"

Sadd said: "She doesn't want coffee, Barry. She just wants you to slow down."

Barry's foot came off the gas pedal. "Sorry, Clara."

I said: "Did you ever see your daughter?"

"Once, when she was an hour old. Never again." He skirted a huge truck and its roar and fumes engulfed us. Now we were past it. "But I knew where she was every month of her life till she got married in 1966 and died a year later, when Beth was born."

I felt a sad little chill at the last words.

Sadd said: "You tracked her?"

"I tracked her."

Now Barry was driving rather too slowly. This was nerve-wracking. Perhaps I shouldn't have encouraged these charged reminiscences while on the road. Well, we'd be in city lock-step in a few minutes.

I said: "By 'tracking' I suppose you mean that you never lost touch with her mother—with Karla."

"By tracking I mean that when Karla left the private hospital I'd put her in, I sent money to get them out of Wiesbaden—all three, Karla, her mother, and the baby—and boarded at a farm in Prenzlau. The mother died the next year, and in 1950 Karla married the farmer. His name was Spenhoff. He was a widower, quite a bit older, but she reported that he was fond of our daughter and they were happy. I sent money for new farm equipment and of course money for Louise's support every year till she was married.''

Sadd said: ''I gather you imposed a certain condition for your daughter's support.''

''Yes, but it was the only one. She was to be told that her father was an American serviceman who had died. The same condition applied to Beth regarding her grandfather.''

''And the same support, no doubt,'' said Sadd dryly.

''Yes, of course. Beth's full name is Elisabeth. It seems Louise worshiped the German movie actress, Elisabeth Bergner.''

The whole thing sounded like a Bergner film, I thought. I said, struggling with chronology: ''Your daughter Louise died when Beth was born. Who else besides Karla in this—this scenario is still living? Beth's father?''

''No.'' Barry grunted. ''Karla gave him a couple of lines in a couple of letters, the gist of them being 'he drank' and later 'he died.' I believe he was a musician of some sort. He remarried after Louise died, a woman with children of her own and Karla didn't like her. I guess it was mutual because Karla raised Beth.''

Sadd said: ''What about Karla's husband, the farmer?''

''Oh, he's long gone.''

Another stretch of silence, then Barry said in a softer voice: ''Karla's been wonderful. Always kept me posted. Her letters would come to my base, wherever I was, and be full of Louise. Later it was Beth she seemed to dote on even more. She'd write things like: 'Elisabeth is so smart, Elisabeth is so beautiful, Elisabeth wants to be a writer.' ''

''Where is Karla now?'' I asked.

''In a retirement home in Frankfurt-am-Main. I wanted the best for her and did some research on the matter when

40

she wrote that she was finding the farmhouse too much. I told her to sell it and invest the money for Beth. I hope Karla's been happy. I think she has. Beth adores her. She sat in my living room the other day and talked about her wonderful grandmother.''

And we were right smack back in the present.

Barry turned east across Central Park as a dozen questions crowded my mind.

Sadd asked one of them: ''How does Beth happen to be in this country?''

Barry chuckled. ''She doesn't just 'happen to be.' '' Then his voice went suddenly flat. ''I'd had a son I'd never seen and a daughter I'd seen once as an infant. I was going to know this grandchild if it was the last thing I did in life.''

''Bravo,'' said Sadd.

''Beth graduated from the University of Augsburg last year, and Karla wrote that she wanted to be a 'newspaper writer.' I told Karla to have her apply to the Columbia School of Journalism, and Beth landed here a month ago for a tour of the country before starting summer classes this June. I was in California at the time, getting myself out of an aeronautics company I've been working for since retiring from the army, and I was scared to death Beth would go home or change universities or whatever before I got back. When I did, a few weeks ago, there was a letter from Karla saying how happy Beth was and that she was improving her English by offering her services at a place called Byways Press.''

Sadd guffawed. ''Presto! You decided to write the life of your grandfather!''

I said reproachfully: ''And you called me up so convincingly to ask about publishers.''

''I had to cover my tracks. Anna was always hovering.''

Anna.

The red glare from the traffic light at Sixty-sixth Street fell across the manila envelope in my lap. Two faces from a time before Beth's mother was born lay in there, neither known to the other, linked by the death of one. Barry turned into Sixty-third Street and pulled up before my door. He turned off his ignition but left his lights on. They lit the row of young trees along the sidewalk. He looked into the street.

"This is where it happened?"

"Yes."

Barry gripped the wheel. "Poor Anna. It's a long time since I loved her, but she sure as hell didn't deserve that."

"No, she didn't." I hadn't been able to take my eyes off the envelope in my lap.

Sadd opened his door. "Thanks for the ride, Barry."

I said: "Why are we assuming that Dollfuss has seen this picture? I'll bet he hasn't."

Sadd closed his door. They both looked at me.

I went on: "We're not sure it ever surfaced till today. Mrs. Hazen said she found it 'in a box' in Anna's apartment. Anna may not have looked in the box in years."

Barry said: "But she was digging up stuff to show Beth, and Dollfuss was there a lot."

"It still doesn't mean this picture ever came to light. I have tons of stuff in boxes I haven't opened in years. I couldn't for the life of me tell you what was in which box."

They admitted the same and we sat in silence for a few seconds, then Sadd opened his door again. Suddenly Barry's fist came down on his horn and it blared in the quiet street.

"Well, by God, I *want* him to see it! And I want him to know *we've* seen it. Especially Beth. She's got to know he is not the guy she thinks he is."

"Now you're talking." I got stiffly out of the car, bewailing my knees. "This picture is a treasure for just one reason: it can help us prove that maybe Dollfuss isn't Dollfuss." I took out my key. "Henry Gamadge had ways of dealing with this sort of thing. I think I'll give a party. Good night, Barry."

In the living room I snapped on some lights and said: "Make us a nightcap, Sadd. Cognac for me. And the bed in the guest room is always made up. I keep a pair of Henry's pajamas in the drawer for gentlemen visitors."

"Do you have many?"

"Certainly. Do not underestimate my elderly charms."

"Name one."

"One charm?"

"One gentleman visitor."

"Well, just last week a college chum of Henry's stayed here. Of course, he brought his wife and his little girl—"

"All right, Mrs. Smarty." He handed me my cognac and we sat down. "Now, what's this about a party? Why a party? What kind of party?"

What kind indeed? I'd said it airily enough, with some thought of getting Dollfuss to my home. But under what pretext? With what witnesses?

"I guess . . . a small dinner party. It will be in honor of Barry and Doris. I'll invite Henry and Tina and Beth and Dollfuss. At some point in the evening I'll produce the picture and we'll see how he reacts. I'm not sure just how I'll produce it. It will have to be casual, apropos of something else—"

"I have an idea. But I haven't been invited to the party."

"I thought you were going to Toronto."

"I can be persuaded to wait a few days. Henry and Tina will put me up if you should have an influx of gentlemen visitors. What night do you have in mind for your dinner party?"

"Let's say Friday. Day after tomorrow. I'll phone everybody. Now, what's your idea?"

Sadd put his drink on the coffee table, planted his short legs apart and leaned forward, his hands on his knees, thoroughly enjoying himself.

"After dinner you start talking about Barry's book—*How Grandpa Saved the Union* or whatever it's called—and you suddenly recall that you recently came across some old photographs of your family, even as far back as your own grandfather, and there may be a Matthew Brady among them—you can't be sure."

"And one of the pictures is of Barry as a cadet! I actually do have one!"

"Splendid. You break out the lot, we have a real nostalgia

43

orgy, and we all watch like hawks when you-know-what appears. Everybody is tipped off except, of course, Beth."

"I love it."

Sadd picked up his drink and sat back in his chair, staring at the glass. He said: "I hope she isn't living with this guy."

"More important, I hope she isn't in love with him."

"That's a fairly cynical statement."

"Sadd, I do not pretend to understand the sexual shenanigans of young people. Good luck to them. All I do know is that Beth and Dollfuss both live in student quarters up on Morningside Drive."

Sadd said: "New York was a hotbed of Nazis in the thirties. Take Yorkville. It was the hatching ground for the bund in this country. Do you realize there could still be elitist groups—"

"I realize it's almost midnight." I stood up and stretched. "I'm usually in bed by nine."

"You don't buy that angle?"

"Somehow, no."

"Granted I was clowning a bit—you did say *fantasize*— that picture makes a Nazi involvement at least logical."

"Yes, it does."

Sadd swallowed his drink and got up and went to the bookcase.

"Let me get a book to take to bed. By the way, where do you suppose Barry got the money to support that ménage in Germany all those years?"

"There's a lot of family money. His father once owned half the real estate in Buffalo. Barry never had to depend on his army pay. Sleep tight."

I left Sadd standing before the bookcase that covered one entire wall of my living room. There were books my husband and I both loved and books he wrote; valuable books and worthless books—except for their contents; books bought for a great deal of money and books bought at yard sales for a quarter; books to save sanity and soul; books it would be impossible to live without.

I myself took Henry Gamadge's *Murderers Speak* off to

bed with me. Sadd had used a word that awakened memory of a line I wanted to read again: "When a motive appears logical, look at it with a very fishy eye."

7

MY DINNER PARTY WAS SHAPING UP NICELY. FRIday proved a good evening for everyone, and I felt quite Machiavellian as I left the phone after briefing my various guests. Tina and Henry, of course, had to be filled in on the discovery of the picture.

Henry said, on the bedroom extension: "Since I don't suppose you plan to prop the thing up on the mantel, how are you going to produce it?"

I explained Sadd's plan.

Tina said, on the kitchen extension: "It's great. We all sit around nonchalantly as this Dollfuss character gets the business. Does the guy in the picture really look that much like him?"

"Absolute image," I said. "It has to be a relative."

"I can't wait. We'll be at your place Friday at five, Clara."

My grandson's voice said into his mother's extension: "Gran, tell Mom not to get a sitter. Please let me come, please!"

The bedroom extension said: "Hen, this is a grown-up dinner party."

I said: "This is a *family* dinner. Of course you can come, dear."

The kitchen extension said: "Go take off those boots—you're making a lake."

I felt sudden alarm. "Did he hear anything we said, Tina?"

"No, I'm sure he didn't. He just this instant got delivered home from the Y."

"Thank goodness. I don't want him to know what's going

46

on. His presence will add a nice touch of innocence. He's only seven, and I want him to keep his image of Gran as a sweet old lady.''

"That may be possible till he's eight," said the bedroom extension.

Barry's reaction was cautious. "Clara, I don't want you taking any chances. If this guy is a killer—"

"He doesn't know we think that."

"True."

"This dinner party is in honor of you and Doris. Even my little grandson will be there. Dollfuss is being invited as a friend of Beth's.''

"That gags me."

"Bring a few chapters of your book. I'll ask you to read and then I'll remember some stuff I have that you might like to use and that will give me an excuse to get out some pictures. *The* picture will be among them, and we'll see how he reacts.''

"*I'll* feel like reacting with a shotgun."

Beth was delighted.

"We would be so pleased to come! I will at once call Dollfuss."

On Friday morning Sadd said he was going down to the New York Public Library and planned to walk the twenty blocks if the weather wasn't "too frigid." I said, looking at my sun-dappled thermometer, that fifty-two degrees was hardly frigid, and he said that the temperature in Florida was probably in the high seventies. I pointed out that low fifties was more salubrious for walking than high seventies, and we ended in our usual draw and Sadd set out.

He returned at noon and walked into the kitchen where I stood surveying a casserole in dismay.

I said: "I should talk about murders. I've just killed this recipe."

47

Sadd shrugged out of his coat. "Cooking never was your strong point, as I recall."

"Sadd, this is serious."

"And how's this for serious: do you realize that in this country since 1960 alone, the Nazi party has—"

"Look at this mess!"

He surveyed the upheaval in the kitchen. "It does look rather like The Day after the Bomb."

Panic seized me. "I haven't attempted a real dinner party since Henry died."

"I strongly recommend a caterer if it isn't too late."

"It is." I racked my brains. "But there's a place on Lexington Avenue Anna always used. They do whole courses. It's sort of a glorified deli."

"Glorious."

"And they deliver."

"Gloriouser and gloriouser."

"You sound like my children. They used to call my cooking 'a rude plenty.'"

I reached for the Yellow Pages, thinking with mortifying clarity of the way in which Tina and my daughter Paula in Boston could whip up fine meals while juggling husbands, children, and jobs. I had no husband, no children now, and never a job, yet I was a kitchen klutz. My face must have reflected my thoughts, for Sadd said casually: "I remember your husband once saying: 'I'd rather have Althea in the kitchen studying a cookbook, and have Clara down in the lab with me studying a signature.'"

How was I supposed to look up a number with wet eyes and no glasses? I pushed the phone book at Sadd and said: "But Althea is gone and Henry is gone and so are all the dear, wonderful days. Find the number for me, please. It's Van Something-or-other on Lexington."

I stared out of the window at the acacia tree, something at least Henry Gamadge and I had looked at together.

Sadd said: "Van Dorn Gourmet Specialties," and started punching numbers.

48

At a quarter to five, needing exercise, I walked to a liquor store on Madison Avenue and taxied back with four bottles of champagne courtesy of Sadd. I arrived at my door as the dinner did. I got the bearer and his pungent burden into the elevator, wrote a check, and instructed him to tell the gentleman upstairs to *touch nothing* till I got there. The buzzer sounded and I let Henry, Tina, and Hen into the hall.

Hen said at once: "Mom said if I go to bed at nine o'clock I can sleep over."

Sleep over! My mind went into reverse. Once when my daughter was seven or eight, I'd read her the Grimm's version of "The Frog Prince," that fairly Freudian tale of the conditions under which the frog will retrieve the Princess's ball from the well: he must be allowed to sit at the table with her and he must sleep in her bed. I'd overheard Paula describing these conditions to a friend the next day: "Then the frog says he wants to stay for supper and sleep over."

I hugged Hen. "You may sleep over forever, darling."

Tina said: "I brought a pie."

"Good. I think I forgot to order dessert."

"Order it?"

I explained the humiliating circumstances of the dinner, and they were unashamedly delighted. Henry, as he never fails to do, stepped from the hallway into his father's laboratory. The closed shutters and shrouded apparatus were untouched since my husband's death.

Henry said: "When are you going to uncover this stuff and do some work?"

"Never."

"Mom, come on!"

"I'm not being morbid. I wouldn't know how." Hen sat in the swivel chair and whirled. "Your father could do nothing in his last years, you know that. And most of this equipment is roughly fifty years old. There have been a few advances in technology since."

"But not necessarily in scholarship," said my son stoutly.

I blew him a kiss. "That was your dad's department. He'd be the one to realize that a Chaucer 'discovery' was probably a fake."

Tina put her pie on the counter and dragged Hen from the swivel chair. She said: "But you could have someone do the lab work. Wasn't there a guy—Harold Somebody—"

"Harold Banz." Dear, loyal, eccentric, gaunt, taciturn Harold, whom Henry Gamadge had literally plucked from the street to become his worhipful lab assistant. "Harold died too," I added. As so many of one's favorite people have a way of doing.

The buzzer sounded and I admitted Barry and Doris. Their presence happily defused the evocations of the room, and we trooped to the elevator.

"Only three at a time," I said, and herded the young Gamadges in, asking Tina to start unboxing the dinner. Then to Barry I spoke the obligatory words of the New York hostess: "Where did you put your car? I meant to tell you there's a garage on Sixtieth that Henry—"

"Yes, he called to tell me." Barry held up a briefcase. "I brought some stuff to lug out on cue. Is Beth here with you-know-who?"

"Not yet. I told them half an hour later."

"Clara, if this guys gets difficult—"

"Barry," Doris put her hand on his arm, "you are not to make a scene. The young man will either react to the picture or he won't, but he will not be difficult, I can almost predict that, can't you, Clara?"

"Yes, I can. He's much too smooth an article." I summoned the elevator. "Remember, Barry, we're just trying to get him into focus. All we do is watch."

"And we have Beth to consider," said Doris. "If she cares for him we have another problem."

Barry fumed at this, and I was glad to get him to the cheerful group above. It was quite like a jolly reunion. Everyone had met, everyone was in on the conspiracy. Tina had unpacked bewilderingly exotic hors d'oeuvres, Sadd tended bar, Barry walked about recalling specific former occasions he'd enjoyed here, and Henry pulled a chair beside his own, instructing Hen to sit there with his "one and only, make it last" Coke. Doris and I finally went into the kitchen, where she said she'd never seen such food and I said I had—on her table. We carried plates into the dining room.

Doris said, looking around at my infinitely old furniture and pictures: "I love this room. How long have you lived here, Clara?"

"Since I was married. And my husband quite some years before that. His parents owned the building."

Doris said, in the kind way people do who think you may be nuts, "I love New York. But I'd be a little afraid to live here."

"Yes, it can be scary." I was setting out silverware. "I guess you have to be a tough old-timer like me. I know New York is a monster. But it's *my* monster."

Tina came in to approve the table with the words: "I'd kill for that Spode."

We debated whether to sit down or to carry plates into the living room.

"I'd say carry," said Doris. "Easier. More informal."

"Mustn't be too formal with murderers." Tina laughed a little but we looked at each other in sudden apprehension, then piled plates at one end of the table.

Sadd called that we should break out the champagne for a toast to the happy couple. We walked back to the living room and I said: "Sadd, we're expecting two more guests, remember?"

This produced a palpable lull, and I took advantage of it. I said:

"Hen, dear, would you like to watch TV in Gran's room? Take those peanuts with you."

Hen departed, conning his mother for a Coke refill, and I

surveyed my fellow conspirators with a twinge of trepidation. I felt suddenly hesitant and nervous, and I tried to say what I had to say without sounding speechifying.

"You know why we're doing this. I think Dollfuss Moltke killed Anna on purpose because of something she knew or had, possibly the letter I've told you about, possibly because of a certain photograph." I went to the desk and picked up a box into which I'd put our Exhibit A plus generous handfuls of old family photographs, large and small. "If the man in the picture is Dollfuss's grandfather—or uncle, or otherwise related—then Dollfuss is not the person he says he is. We're going to try to surprise him into some sort of reaction or acknowledgment when he sees it."

Tina said: "Do we know if Beth has seen the picture?"

Barry's voice was a little harsh. "If she has, she can't have taken in its real significance. Tonight I—we intend she shall." Then his grim face lightened; he seemed to remember his role as mere avuncular acquaintance. "I'm anxious to protect that nice young lady. I've become very fond of her."

I drowned a spurt of compassion for Barry with a sip of my drink and went on: "What I thought we might do is this: after dinner I'll tell Barry we'd like to hear a few chapters of the book he's writing about his grandfather."

Sadd groaned and Barry said: "Quiet, Saddlier, or I'll read the whole damn thing."

Doris hid a smile, and Henry and Tina, not being apprised of the reason for the memoir, looked a little startled at this exchange.

I went hastily on: "Then I'll say something to the effect that I recently came across some old photographs and I recall that Barry appears in some of them and maybe he'd like to have them for his book. Henry, you say you'd all like to see them, and the rest of you pipe up yes, you would, and Sadd, I'll ask you to get out the card table—it's in the hall closet—and I'll dump the pictures out and we'll all paw through them and at some point this one will surface."

I opened the box and extracted the fateful picture. I handed

52

it to Tina, saying: "I think you and Henry are the only ones who haven't seen it."

They stared at it, fascinated.

The buzzer sounded.

8

THE PAIR OF DAZZLING YOUNG CREATURES
walking through my door looked more than ever like Sig-
mund and Sieglinde. Their two heads shone gold above Beth's
blue dress and Dollfuss's dark blazer. I found it difficult to
look into his face, remembering the last time I'd seen it.

Beth carried a white box, which she presented to Doris
with a kiss. "I wiss"—that rare lapse in her pronunciation—
"that I could be at the wedding, but I will be back in Germany on that day."

I didn't dare look at Barry. Doris quickly pulled the ribbon
from the box and produced, amid appreciative comments, a
charming vase.

"You're abandoning our opus, Beth?" Barry spoke with
admirable lightness.

"Only for a short while. I want to see my grandmother.
I've told you about her, have I not? She's in a home of retirement in Frankfurt. I haven't seen her since I came to the
States, and she is in her eighties. Then I will come back in
time for my summer classes."

Barry beamed his relief upon her, and I said: "Well, we're
glad you're here now to drink a wedding toast with us. Sadd,
will you do the honors?"

Dollfuss said: "Mrs. Gamadge, I believe I have not met
these nice people." I apologized and introduced him to
Henry and Tina and then to Hen, who came in from the
bedroom to stare at the golden creatures and to be given a
good-natured lesson in the pronunciation of the name "Dollfuss" by its owner. Doris and Sadd and I passed the cham-

54

pagne, and Beth sat down beside Barry and said: "You must work hard on your book, Colonel, while I'm gone. You hardly need me at all, you know, you are such an excellent writer. Mr. Saddlier," she accepted a glass from him, "do you know why Colonel Lockwood chose me to help him from among all the people at Byways Press?"

Sadd said: "I'd guess it had something to do with your scholarly appearance, your plain face, your sensible shoes—"

"He said," Beth laughed up at him, "that he might someday write about his own military career, and that as I was born and brought up in Germany where he did service, we might get acquainted and work on that book later."

I felt rather a desire to cry, and at the same time gratitude to Beth for the perfect opening.

"Oh, that reminds me! Barry has brought some chapters from his book. Won't it be a treat to hear them after dinner?"

Up went a dutiful chorus of assent.

A hostess's lot is not a happy one, happy one, I sang to myself as, longing to eavesdrop on Barry's conversation with Dollfuss, whom he had cornered, I must needs flit about to pass this and pour that. Doris and Henry were swapping awed stories about the price of real estate in the Berkshires, Sadd was trumpeting that the place to buy property was Florida, and Tina and Beth were discussing a play they'd both seen. At one point Hen spilled something in the kitchen, which took me out of the room for seven or eight minutes, and then I got him settled back in the bedroom in front of the television with a Popsicle. When I returned to the party, groupings had changed and dessert was in progress.

Beth said: "Mrs. Gamadge, never have I had such a supper. You must let us help you with the dishes."

"Absolutely not. But you may all carry your stuff out to the kitchen and leave it there. Then I've planned something much more interesting than washing dishes."

"Colonel Lockwood's book," said loyal son Henry.

"And a surprise of my own." I smiled, I hoped mysteriously. "Sadd, will you get the card table? It's in the hall closet."

Sadd said: "Clara, if we're going to play cards, you know I hate—"

"Who said anything about cards?" I knew Sadd was enjoying this charade and I hoped he wasn't going to overdo it. "Just put the table up and I'll show you something I think you'll all enjoy, especially Barry."

They trooped back and forth to the kitchen with their plates and I went to the desk with beating heart. Sadd flipped open the legs of the card table and set it squarely in the middle of the room. Now they were all back and Doris said:

"I know. Parlor games."

"Clara, I loathe them." This from Barry.

"Card tricks," said Tina.

"Mother!" Henry looked at me aghast. "If you're going to start asking us where the ace of spades is—"

"Will you shush?" I was getting downright nervous. Beth and Dollfuss were listening to this badinage with half-smiling, half-bewildered looks. I'd better get on with it before my accomplices got carried away.

I said: "I came across this box of old pictures just the other day when I was looking for something else, and I had a wonderful, weepy time going through it. When Beth said she and Barry might be working on his own memoirs, I thought of one picture in particular."

I lifted the lid, fumbled, as I had practiced doing, through the pictures, drew out a charming photograph of eighteen-year-old Barry resplendent in cadet's uniform, and held it up.

The surprise, the laughter, and the applause were totally genuine. Doris reached for it automatically and lovingly.

"Oh, Clara, may I have it?"

"Of course."

The picture was passed, admired, kidded about—"That Nathan Hale expression!" said Sadd—and ended up in Doris's possession. The moment was so pleasant that I felt a little ashamed of what was to follow.

Henry said: "Any more as good as that?"

"Oh, lots. Would you like to see them?"

Up went the chorus again, with Beth and Dollfuss joining ̣. "Then pull up chairs."

I emptied the contents of the box on the table and the ̣ctures splayed out, covering it. It was instant fun. I'd care- lly maneuvered my bomb to the bottom of the pile, and for ̣ree or four minutes the actors in my drama seemed to forget ̣at there was one. Hilarity, recognition, and nostalgia ̣igned.

"Clara, you look like Minnie Pearl in that hat!"

"Henry, you were *fat*!"

"I was not. I was healthy."

"Sadd, if I had a Nathan Hale expression, you had an instein one."

"I still have that cap and gown!"

"This says 'Clara, Confirmation Day.' "

"Was I not an angelic-looking child?"

"Deceivingly so."

"Nauset Beach! Will you ever forget those horseflies?"

The merriment had drawn Hen from the bedroom. "Gee, ̣ncle Sadd, I didn't know you were in the army."

"Air Force. Watch your language, young man."

"Mrs. Gamadge, what a pretty dress."

"Remember those, Doris? Short in back and long in ̣ont."

"Yes, you looked as if someone had taken a pair of shears ̣ you."

The picture was working its way to the surface. It lay just ̣neath my daughter in her wedding dress. I lifted that and ̣ld it up. "My lovely daughter."

"My lovely sister," said Henry.

The picture lay on top. Beth picked it up and read: "Olym-̣c Games, Germany, 1936." She peered closer. "Why, ̣olonel Lockwood, that's you!"

Barry took the picture from her. "It sure is." He looked me in surprise. "Clara, where on earth did you get this?"

"Who knows? Anna probably gave it to me."

Dollfuss said: "Nineteen thirty-six? Was that not the yea of the great win of Jesse Owens?"

"I believe it was," said Barry. "Are you a sports devo tee?"

"My father and grandfather were. I was brought up on th records of great athletes."

Hen's voice coming over Barry's shoulder was clear: "Tha guy looks like *you*, Dollfuss."

As Tina said later, when you're engaged in skullduggery you invite children at your peril. Beth took the picture from Barry and said:

"What guy . . . ? Oh, yes. It does rather, Dolly."

But Dollfuss was studying another picture. "What charming bride you were, Mrs. Gamadge."

Hen scuttled behind Beth and took the picture from her He said: "Are these guys soldiers?"

Dollfuss, seated beside Beth, looked up now at the pictur and at Hen. He said: "Yes, but not the kind you have in you country."

"Or ever hope to have," said Barry.

Back went the picture under the nose of Dollfuss to Beth

"What's that uniform, Dolly? The SS?"

"I believe so."

"Yes." Barry reached for it and the picture made its thir trip past Dollfuss. "The infamous SS." He laughed a little "By golly, there is a resemblance, Dollfuss. Hope he's n relation—for your sake."

But Dollfuss was smiling and holding up for all to see picture of my son at one year, seated on a wicker contraptio I'd found in his grandparents' attic.

"I would recognize you even at this age, Mr. Gamadge but explain please the meaning of where you are seated." Dollfuss read from the bottom of the picture: "Henry Ju nior, one year old on potty chair."

It was impossible not to laugh, and I knew it was over Tina stood up and took the picture from Dollfuss. "Oh, have to have that one. Hen, if you want to stay at Gran's, sa good night."

58

She walked with him to the guest bedroom door, which led off the living room, and we all waved.

Sadd said: "My quarters have been usurped. You're stuck with me tonight, Henry."

"Fine with us. Colonel, when do we get to hear that chapter?"

Oh, thank you, dear boy. Everybody stood up and helped assemble the pictures as I went to the kitchen to make more coffee. Dollfuss followed me. He said he'd been of no use all evening and he'd be glad to start the dishes while the Colonel got out his manuscript. I said I had a dishwasher, and Dollfuss said it was his ambition to own one some day.

Had we been nuts? Was the resemblance indeed just a freaky happenstance? The whole episode had taken less than a minute and not made a ripple. My elaborate drama had gained us nothing. What had I really expected anyway? I wasn't sure now. The others were deflated too, I could tell, as we sat down again and Dollfuss passed the coffee.

Barry said: "Doris and I have a long trip home so I'll just read a few pages—in fact, maybe just the introduction, because Beth suggested it."

He read, with nice simplicity, the account of a young Scottish lad who had come to this country with his parents in the year 1860. They had settled in Providence, Rhode Island, and on his twenty-second birthday he had done two things: married a beautiful girl and enlisted in the Union army. There followed what he always told his children and grandchildren was "perhaps not the perfect honeymoon."

We laughed and applauded and Barry said it would never have occurred to him to start the book so appealingly but that Beth had thought of it after listening to some of his tales. Beth said she thought the Colonel's grandfather sounded like a delightful man, and it came to me dimly that she was speaking of her own great-great-grandfather, but I was too tired and let down to contemplate this touching fact for long.

Now they were all leaving. Tina went into the bedroom to check on Hen, who was sound asleep. She said she'd come for him next day, she wanted to go to Macy's anyway. The

59

elevator made three or four trips and everyone said I was not to come down and I didn't. Last to go were Beth and Dollfuss. I wished her a safe trip and a happy visit with her grandmother.

I was alone. I walked to the desk and looked at the box lying there with its contents replaced. I opened it and dumped the pictures on the desk. With the image of Dollfuss so fresh in my mind, I'd take a last look, then try to forget the matter.

The picture was gone.

I threw everything on the floor, knowing as I did there could be no mistake; it had been the biggest of the lot. I looked around in something of a daze. Under a piece of furniture, wafted there in the repacking? Even as I searched I told myself the thing had left with Dollfuss. I gathered everything up and somehow got it all back in the desk drawer. My hands were shaking rather too badly to manage the box lid.

The buzzer sounded.

Which of my guests had forgotten what? Still dazed, I did what I had never done before and what no one in New York City ever does—especially at night! I pressed the speaker and the door button together.

"Mrs. Gamadge, this is Dollfuss. Thank you. I won't stay long."

Oh, God—oh, God! I'd let a murderer into my house with my grandson asleep there.

9

WEAK WITH HORROR, I MADE MY HAND REACH
for the button that summoned the elevator. That would give
me extra seconds to think. I addressed God sternly: let anything happen to that child and You and I are through. He
addressed me back: use your head, there's a lock on that
bedroom door.

Oh, thank You! I ran with shaking knees to the desk, hearing the elevator start down. I grabbed the key and got it into
the lock I'd had put on the door to safely enclose my husband's rare books when I rented my place. I sank the key
into a plant on the windowsill and was walking across the
room as the elevator appeared and Dollfuss emerged from
it.

We stood and looked at each other, then he said: "I have
come back for the picture."

I said stupidly: "Picture?"

"The one of Colonel Lockwood at the games that also
contains my grandfather. May I have it, please?"

I was not faking bafflement. My mind was a true blank.
The picture. The one I was sure he'd stolen. He'd come back
for it. He came a little farther into the room and said, almost
kindly: "You're very tired after your nice dinner party. If I
may have the picture, please, I'll go at once."

I backed into a chair and sat down looking up at this slender, Teutonic apparition. I said: "I'm not sure I want to part
with it."

"Then I will simply have to take it."

Dollfuss walked to the desk and picked up the empty box. He said: "Where is it, please?"

It was the third or fourth "please" since he'd appeared. The gentleman thief. I said: "The whole bunch is in the top drawer, but the one you want is gone. I assumed you'd taken it."

"I wish I had. I wish I had." His voice trembled. "In that picture my grandfather is the age that I am now. He was my hero and I have no picture of him. Of course, you've hidden it."

I was beginning to recover from the shock of his reappearance, but the shock of his changed manner and bewildering demand was harder to absorb. I said the first thing that occurred to me.

"Dollfuss, why would I hide it?"

My use of his name seemed to do something to his shoulders.

"To use against me."

"In what way?"

"You know, of course. But my grandfather was never brought to trial. After Nuremburg he killed himself in prison. Heroically. Gloriously."

He looked at me in defiance, waiting for me to speak. For the life of me I couldn't. Then he said: "Now I will find the picture."

First the desk drawers, then with swift precision he moved around the room. From my chair I watched, mesmerized. In magazines, behind sofa cushions, under corners of the rug. Would he find it? Had the true culprit hidden it somewhere in the room? He ran his hand behind the books in the bookshelf, and at one point stood still, his hands in his shining hair, and said, as if alone and thinking aloud: "Certainly in this room. Not enough time between my ringing and my entering to take it far, and I was not expected back."

"You sure weren't." I realized, to my relief, that I sounded both fearless and severe. "May I ask how you managed to separate yourself from Beth? Or does she know you're here?"

"She does not." Dollfuss opened an atlas and flicked the

62

ages. "The Colonel suggested she go home with them to work on his book tomorrow. I walked to the corner, then back."

He stood before me, and at close range his eyes were frightening.

He said: "Get up, please." Another "please." I hastened to obey, and he threw the cushions of my chair on the floor. Standing in the middle of the room I saw his eyes go to the door of the guest bedroom. As a child I once rolled over on a feather bed in my aunt's cottage on Cape Cod; the feeling of suffocation returned to me in a wave. I said:

"Dollfuss, you know that my grandson is asleep in there. Have you ever heard the American expression 'over my dead body?' "

"No."

"It means you would have to kill me to get in there—and to no purpose, I solemnly assure you."

He shrugged. "You would not have needed to go out of the room with it. Do you have any whiskey?"

"Yes," I said, relief engulfing me.

I walked into the kitchen and he followed me. I looked longingly at the wall phone. If Dollfuss felled me where I stood, who would know? Barry and Doris and Beth were still hours from Lake Winifred, but Tina, Henry, and Sadd were nearing Brooklyn Heights, perhaps already there.

I pointed to a cabinet over the refrigerator and Dollfuss took down a bottle of bourbon. We both looked around the kitchen, still in disarray, and he must have thought, as I did, that our conversation about dishwashers had taken place in another life. I walked out of the kitchen; Dollfuss could find a clean glass. I'd be darned if I'd play hostess to a crazy intruder.

My living room had been upended. I felt more angry than afraid now. I said as he came in: "You've made a mess in here to no avail. At least have the courtesy to tell me why you didn't acknowledge the man in the photo as your grandfather while everyone was here."

Dollfuss took a long pull on his bourbon. "Because the

63

SS was feared and despised. Even Beth might have been shocked. Her sympathies are very western. Did you know her grandfather was an American? She admires your culture, whereas I consider it . . ." He thought for a moment, then smiled. "Yes. A word I learned recently: flabby. The Third Reich was, as you must realize, the most magnificent period in the history of the world." Another defiant look—glare, actually. "And, of course, the writing on the back had shocked you."

On the back? On the back? On the back of what?

"It was such a thrilling surprise to see it," Dollfuss went on, sipping his drink as if he was at a party. "I'm told I look very much like my grandfather, and I have no picture of him in his prime. One was here tonight and it was snatched from me." He looked around moodily. "To see what was written there—and then to lose it!"

My head buzzed. In all the handling and shuffling and scrutinizing of that picture, not one of us had thought to turn it over. What could Anna have written? When had she written it? In 1936? Last week? I said to myself: let that alone, Clara, or you'll go nuts. Aloud I said: "Had you ever seen the picture before?"

"Never."

"When did you see what was written on the back?"

"When the little boy took it from me. He was standing behind me holding it and I looked up. That was a moment of great elation."

Dollfuss had started to wander around the room again, turning over this book and opening that drawer, but the impetus of the hunt had gone out of him. Would I get my come-uppance now, the result of tipsy disappointment? I said: "Now, *I* need a drink."

I started back to the kitchen, expecting him to follow me. Instead he sat down on the sofa and said: "The picture is not here. I know who has taken it."

I stopped, intrigued. "You do?"

"Colonel Lockwood. He wishes to discredit me with Beth. He need not trouble. Tomorrow I return to Germany."

"Not to Austria?"

"To Germany. My homeland."

The phone rang. I was ten feet from the kitchen extension. I flew to it.

Sadd's voice said: "Good, you're still up. We just got in and I had to 'rap' with you, as the kids say. It's slangy but effective, and 'rap' has a valid—"

"Sadd, I have a gentleman visitor."

Pause. "Don't tell me I've interrupted a tryst. Clara, at your age—"

"It's Dollfuss."

"My God."

"He just came back to thank me for the dinner because he's going away and we won't see him again." Dollfuss stood in the door. "Yes, of course I'll look for your glasses. Don't apologize, I'm forever leaving mine behind too. Dollfuss is just leaving. Call back in fifteen minutes. I'm sure I'll find them."

I hung up and said: "Mr. Saddlier insists he isn't getting forgetful but the truth is—"

"I will go now."

"Please do." My relief at Sadd's call suddenly crumbled into resentment that Dollfuss was walking jauntily away with Anna unavenged.

He reached for the bottle of bourbon. "Perhaps—an expression of your country I have heard—'one for the road' before I am attempting your underground transportation."

He poured a generous slug and drank it slowly but steadily. He was curiously elated, and not, I felt, entirely because of the liquor. There had been an undercurrent of elation about him from the start, even during his fruitless search. Whatever Dollfuss had come to this country to do or get, he'd done it or gotten it and was returning home triumphant *and* with the letter he'd killed Anna for. I felt a rising rage but tried to keep my voice steady.

"Dollfuss, you'll be gone tomorrow, out of the country, out of the lives of all of us. Answer this question: why did Anna Pitman have to die?"

He put his glass down on the kitchen counter with a small bang. "Ah, that unhappy lady! Perhaps it was best."

"What was best?"

"The accident."

"Perhaps it wasn't an accident."

I expected him to flare, indignant with denial. Instead he nodded sadly. "Possibly you are right. Possibly she did indeed throw herself under my car."

"You murderous, lying bastard!"

Had this appalling shout come from me? Through the pounding in my head I heard his laugh—why was it worse than anger?—and he said:

"What a so faithful friend to the poor suspicious Anna! Now I will go."

"Damn right!"

Really, Clara, you'd better just simmer down and try to remember you're a lady. I stalked past him and pulled open the elevator gate.

"No need for you to come down," said Dollfuss politely.

I motioned him in and followed. I had to know that he was really gone; there were doors off the shadowy hall below. Thank God for our mutual knowledge that Sadd was hanging over a phone in Brooklyn counting those fifteen minutes. In the elevator our clothing touched. You don't stand in close confines with someone who believes the Third Reich was the Golden Age without a certain tightening of the throat—especially if you have just called him a murderer. Or had that been a compliment?

I switched on the hall light and we walked side by side to the front door. Through my rage and frustration a gnawing curiosity on a small point was making itself felt. If I couldn't get satisfaction in a large matter, at least perhaps I could in a small one. I opened the door and said:

"I have a last question, *Dolly*."

He reacted to my deliberate, mocking use of his pet name with a quick stare over his shoulder as he stepped into the street.

66

"Why would your grandfather want you named for an enemy of the Reich?"

No laugh this time. The streetlight—I'm blessed with one at my door—caught three-quarters of his spectacular face, and it froze in the expression of rage I'd expected to see when I'd accused him of the worst of all crimes.

"My name is not Dollfuss! My people detested him! 'Dolly' is from childhood, short for my real name—Adolf!— the name of my grandfather's *true* hero!"

He walked away.

Spent and depressed, I went back upstairs, then hurried to the guest bedroom, the doorknob of which was rattling as a plaintive voice called that it was stuck and I have to go to the bathroom. I released my grandson as the phone rang. Hen picked up the receiver at the desk.

"Hello, this is Henry Gamadge. Oh, hi, Dad. I have to go to the bathroom. What's the matter?"

I seized the receiver and pushed the beloved little shoulders in their sagging tee-shirt toward the hall. Then I addressed the squawkings from all three extensions in Brooklyn.

"Calm down, all of you. Tina, darling, stop crying—Hen's okay. Yes, I understand your panic and I'm sorry I caused it. Come to think of it, I didn't. Sadd, you idiot, why did you even tell them?"

"I forgot about Hen," said Sadd contritely.

Henry said, quoting his father's favorite line after a crisis: "All's well that ends well. What did Dollfuss come back for, Mom?"

"For the picture of his grandfather who was his hero."

They all exclaimed something in unison to the effect that we'd been right.

"Did you give it to him?" asked Sadd.

"It was gone."

"Gone?" said the three voices.

"Disappeared. Missing. Did any of you take it?"

"Take it?" said three voices.

"You sound like a Greek chorus. Go to bed. I'll explain all tomorrow. Dollfuss, whose real name is Adolf, is gone too, back to his homeland, and I guess we'll have to let him go." I'm sure I sounded bitter; I felt bitter. "Your son wants something to eat. Good night."

Half an hour later Hen was asleep again, but reader (as Charlotte Brontë would say), you will empathize with my kind of night: fitful dozes, frightful dreams; out to the living room for a book; into the kitchen to make tea; snap on the television to be sold jewelry, salvation, and fingernails; back to bed, up for the bathroom, back to bed. Finally, dead asleep, wakened by the phone.

"Clara, this is Barry. I know it's early but I have to talk to you."

Mumble.

"Damn, I woke you up. I'll call later."

"Barry, wait—did you take that picture?"

"What picture? Oh, you mean—no, why would I take it? Is it gone?"

"Talk to you later. Let me sleep."

That left only one other person. Back to sleep to be wakened by One Other Person, her voice scarcely audible.

"Mrs. Gamadge, please help me, oh, please help me. I had to call—I have to see you—I'm so frightened."

Groggily: "Beth, where are you?"

"At Doris's. She says I can borrow her car. She'll tell the Colonel that I remembered other work I must do. Please let me come, but not to your house. I will be at the Empire Diner on Tenth—"

"I know the place." I was struggling to come to.

"—and there is someone I want you to meet. Oh, Mrs. Gamadge—"

"Beth, slow down."

I hadn't taken in everything the scared young voice had said except for Barry not being let in on the reason—whatever it was—for her flight. That appealed to me. Poor Doris, with her wedding less than a week away, had been a sufficiently good sport about all this. She was probably relieved to be delivering the girl into my hands before Barry could go into

68

his Mother Hen act again. Beth was murmuring, "So sorry, sorry, oh, so frightened—"

"Beth, of course you can come, but why do we have to traipse all the way down—"

"Because Dollfuss might be waiting for me at your place or at my room or at Byways. And because there is someone I want you to meet."

Ah, yes. That phrase had swept past me in the course of her first outburst. Someone she wanted me to meet.

"Will this someone be at the Empire?"

"Just up the street at the Chelsea Hotel."

I felt instant respect for Someone. The Chelsea, on Twenty-third Street, had been one of Henry Gamadge's favorite places, a home, a refuge, a hangout for writers. I said, getting my feet on the floor and kicking about in quest of slippers: "Dollfuss came back last night for that picture you took."

A gasp. "Oh, Clara!"

I smiled, touched by the fact that in panic and need she had called me Clara. I said: "The man in it was his grandfather and he's very proud of it."

"You see what he is! You see what he is!" Her voice shook.

"Is it because of the picture you're afraid of him?"

"Oh, before that! Was he angry to find it gone?"

"Yes, but he thinks Colonel Lockwood took it. Bring it with you. There's something written—"

"Oh, dear. I slipped it into the Colonel's briefcase."

Damn. And Barry must be spared knowledge of her departure. I felt like the victim of some refined Oriental torture.

"Beth," I started to say—then broke off, staring at the rumpled figure of my grandson, whose presence in the house I'd completely forgotten. I held out my arms.

"Darling, come here. I am a *rotten* granny."

"Will you make pancakes?"

"You bet I will. Beth, my grandson is still here and I'll have to wait till his mother comes for him. It will take you at least three hours to get to Manhattan. Shall we say two o'clock at the Empire Diner?''

''Oh, thank you, thank you!''

''I don't know where you'll be able to put Doris's car. I've never been to the Chelsea district except by subway or bus.''

''My friend at the hotel will take care of it for me. Oh, Clara, I'll never forget this.''

Neither will I, I thought grimly as I hung up and asked Hen to find my slippers, which in the course of last night's thrashings seemed to have vanished. He dove under the bed and produced them and we went to the kitchen to make pancakes.

10

WHEN I'D MOPPED UP SYRUP AND MOPPED UP Hen and turned down the decibel rating of the TV cartoons, I poured a glass of orange juice, wrestled with myself for all of three seconds before putting a shot of vodka in it, got back into bed and called Doris.

I said: "What the heck happened?"

"Clara, I don't know."

"Was it Barry's idea to take Beth home with you?"

"Yes, and she seemed anxious to come. She could do a lot of organizing of material, she said, and have it ready for him to work on while she was in Germany. Then this morning she couldn't wait to take off again! Hold on—my cat's on the kitchen counter. Let me grab him."

I held on, envying her grabbing him. I'd lost a beloved, elderly cat the year before. Now Doris was back.

"When we left your place, Barry remembered he had an appointment with his lawyer in New York this morning, so he decided to stay at a hotel and Beth and I drove home. She became very quiet and hardly spoke at all. In fact, she suddenly seemed to be in a state of mild shock. When we got here she went right to bed—then at the crack of dawn she was shaking me and saying she had to see you right away, could she borrow my car and would I make some excuse to Barry when he got home."

"Doris," I said, "you don't need this on practically your wedding eve. And I hope she gets that car back to you."

"No rush. I drive Barry's more often than not. And I'd rather this than have him get all riled up again."

"Amen to that. Why don't you tell him you've always dreamed of getting married in Greece and leave tomorrow?"

She laughed and I told her she was a saint.

At noon Tina arrived to pick up Hen and to say she'd just driven Sadd to the airport for his visit to his daughter's family in Toronto. Kathy was an entirely pleasant, country-clubbish young woman, her husband was an entirely pleasant, country-clubbish young man, and their little girls entirely unpleasant, pretty, prodigiously spoiled twins.

I said: "There must have been other ways you could have spent a precious Saturday morning besides dragging to the airport. Thank you, Tina."

"Well, I did tell Henry it's his turn next. I give the visit three days."

I said, "I'm having lunch with Beth, but not here. She's mortally afraid Golden Boy will be looking for her."

"Why afraid?"

"Heaven knows, Tina. I suppose she'll tell me. What's wrong?"

Hen was having his lunch at the kitchen table. Tina had declined any and was seated beside him nibbling his potato chips. Her hand was shaking a little.

She said: "Clara, other than Dollfuss—or whatever his name is—acknowledging it to you in private, is there any other way the man in the picture can be proved to be his grandfather? I mean," she looked distressed, "if this is a bad scene, and you're the only one who knows, and you should . . ."

"Should find myself in the path of that big old red Buick, is that what you mean?"

"Yes."

I put my hand on hers. "Not to worry, dear. Beth told me last night she sold it."

She laughed, choking a little. "You know perfectly well what I mean."

"Of course I do. Actually, there seems to be some sort of clincher about the picture. Something written on the back. Lord knows why none of us thought to turn the thing over."

"Written? Who wrote it?"

"Anna, presumably. The picture was never out of her possession all those years. Anyway, Beth tucked it into Barry's briefcase, so we'll have to wait till we can get it back. Beth didn't want to involve Barry any further, and Doris . . ." My voice trailed with the realization that I'd said enough.

"And Doris doesn't need this trip laid on her," said Tina dryly. She went to the hall closet for Hen's coat. "As it is, she's being pretty understanding about Barry's protégé, isn't she?"

I tried to think of something loyal and nonrevealing and came up feebly with, "Fortunately, she's no Anna."

Tina said: "I must admit, Beth is a terrific girl. Those foreign students are always so damn *bright*. Do you realize she also speaks French and Italian?"

"And what she calls 'a little Spanish,' which probably means she could write a book in it."

"How did she ever get tied up with that son-of-a-Nazi?"

"I intend to find out today."

At one o'clock I took the Fifth Avenue bus down to Twenty-second Street and walked through the grimily lovely spring over to Tenth Avenue. Before the silvery exterior of the Empire Diner stood Beth, her blue dress of last night rumpled under a raincoat. Her hair was tied back with a plaid ribbon, the first time I had seen it not flowing. The effect was severe but, inevitably, lovely. She ran to me.

"I feel so safe now. I sall pay for the lunch." The funny little slip, tension apparent in her face. "You muzz let me."

"Okay."

We went in and took a table at the extreme right end of the diner. A landmark of sorts, the art nouveau of the spotless place makes one feel that Scott and Zelda might have stumbled in for coffee that morning at dawn. The traffic on Tenth Avenue streams by its door, which is never closed.

It was a good hour for privacy. Except for three people at the counter, we were alone. And a good thing too. Beth picked up the menu, stared at it and said: "Of course you know that he killed Anna not by accident but on purpose."

My elbow skidded along the shiny surface of the table and sent my knife and spoon spinning. The approaching waitress picked them up, gave me others, and stood waiting for the order.

Beth said: "I think the sandwich and the soup. What is it?"

"Clam chowder."

I said: "The same." I'd have said "the same" if Beth had ordered a haunch of venison; my eyes weren't taking in the menu too well. When the waitress departed I managed a few words. "How do you know?"

"I saw him do it."

I remembered the knife and spoon problem and planted my hands in my lap. If we were going to have soup I'd darn well better know where my elbows were.

Beth leaned forward. "And you saw him too."

I was truly speechless and could only stare back at her. Her eyes slid from mine out of the window to where a taxi driver was arguing with his fare on the pavement. She went on agitatedly: "Why do you suppose I brought that car to poor Anna's service? I wanted you to see it, to be shocked, to remember." Now she looked back at me. "Colonel Lockwood has told me, from the first time I met you, so often you help with things that are—are full of fear, frightful—what is the word—fright . . . ?"

"Frightening. Beth, calm down, please. You say you saw the—the thing happen"—now I too was stumbling—"and you saw me. Where were you?"

"On the sidewalk, a few yards from you only." She drew a shaky breath and gulped some water. Our soup arrived. We both looked at it blankly. I said:

"Tell me exactly what happened—from the beginning."

"I left Byways Press with Dollfuss—"

"Don't call him that!"

It was involuntary and I could have bitten my tongue.

74

Wide, scared eyes. "Why?"

"It isn't his name. But never mind that now—go on."

"No—tell me." She reached for my hand, which I'd let stray to the tabletop.

I told her and we clung together.

"Of course, of course." Her voice shook. "The name Dollfuss fits with the little name on the picture."

"And with his Austrian image."

Her hand was freezing. I pulled mine gently away and said: "Get some of that hot chowder into you before you say another word."

Beth picked up her spoon, then laid it down again.

"No, I muzz tell you. We said we would pick up Anna and take her home. Colonel Lockwood gave us your address and we started downtown. I let Doll—I let him drive. I always did. He loved to. The rain was very bad and he said perhaps when we got to your street I should get out, since it would be impossible to park, and go in and tell Anna we were there while he drove around the block and then we could be waiting for him when he came back. I got out at the corner of Madison Avenue"—her breath was coming in little gasps—"and ran toward your house and I saw Anna standing in the door with you. Then I saw her run out, and then I saw what he did . . . and I thought—I knew—you had seen it too."

I looked down at my chowder. I was incapable of swallowing, and Beth had pushed hers to one side.

"I saw your two friends come out and take you back into your house. The police came very soon. His upset—upsetness—is that a word?—was very good. His license must have been in order, though he did not let me see it when he showed it—for of course it was German, not Austrian, and contained his real name. Then many people said how bad the day was for skidding and he said that the lady was a friend he had come to pick up and he could not believe his bad fortune. Next day I went with him to the police station and said yes, the car was mine and I had been with him and had asked him to drive, and they said Anna's only relative had made no trouble—no, there's another word—"

"Charges."

"Charges. And there was the end."

I'd been listening to this account with my mind snagged on the old question. I said: "Beth, *why*?"

She looked at me in surprise. "But surely it is now clear. Anna had discovered him. No—I'm close—"

"Uncovered?"

"Ah." Beth drew her soup back. She appeared purged by her account.

"You mean because of the picture?"

"Certainly."

I shook my head. "It won't wash."

"Won't . . . ?"

"Just an expression. How long have you known—"

"No, please." She reached for her enormous bag and took out a notebook. "I want always to understand these expressions. 'Won't wash'?"

"It just means something doesn't make sense. Dollfuss— we might as well call him that, it comes easier than his real name—never saw that picture till last night. And I'll bet Anna hadn't looked at it in years. There has to be another reason." Why distract her with mention of the letter? I craved answers I at least knew I could get.

"How long have you known this guy, Beth?"

"A few weeks." Beth had started on her soup and I made an attempt to do the same. "He has a room in my building. He came a little after I did. We thought he was a student also but he said he was just seeing the sights of this country. Of course, his good looks make him of great appeal. Every girl in the place is mad about him. But he seems . . ."

"To prefer you. I can't imagine why."

"Well, of course, the language."

"Why, sure—that's it."

"I did wonder at his accent, but he said he had been to school in Germany. Then I introduced him to my friend at the Chelsea Hotel, the one I want you to meet. The man I hope to marry.''

Marry. Beth hoped to marry the Someone at the Chelsea Hotel. That was the end of the soup. I put down my spoon and simply looked at her. Leave that alone for the moment, Clara. Back up and get things in sequence.

"Beth, listen to me: whatever the reason Dollfuss did what he did, you and I are the only ones who know what we saw, and it's too late to do anything about it. He's going back to Germany and—"

"He told you that?" She looked up eagerly.

"Today, he said. And we have to let him go."

Beth went back to her soup rather energetically. "Oh, that is relief. That is great relief. He returns to his friends, so many young men who dream of those terrible days with pride. I think"—she stared at her spoon—"that he knows I saw what he did, though I never said a word—I was too afraid. I shall not be now, and you shall not be either. I was worried for you also. But he would not ever dare to risk another 'accident.' He is leaving." Beth drew a breath. "He is leaving." She started on her sandwich.

Okay, Clara. Ready for the next round? I said: "Now tell me about the man you plan to marry."

"Plan? Oh, if I *could* plan! But for now I can only hope."

I was not in the mood for lovelorn vapors. "You said he knows Dollfuss?"

"Yes, I introduced them. Albrecht thought Dollfuss was splendid. Now he will be horrified."

"Albrecht? He's German too?"

She nodded. "And the nicest part is, he knows my grandmother."

My elbows skidded again, but this time only mentally. Beth was chowing down on her sandwich. I said I thought I'd doggy bag mine and out came the notebook again.

"Yes, I have heard that expression. It means—"

"It means most Americans' eyes are too big for their stomachs." I ordered coffee and decided to let Albrecht go for the moment in favor of some background exploring. I wanted to add what I could to Barry's skeletal account.

"Tell me something about yourself, Beth. Where were you brought up?"

"In Prenzlau, by my grandmother. My mother died when I was born and my father married again. He married a woman with children of her own and they lived in Bavaria somewhere. He was a musician, but I believe he drank a great deal, and then he too died." The sandwich was disappearing fast. "My grandfather was an American soldier and my grandmother says they were married, but I strongly do not believe her. What does it matter? I am very proud of my American blood."

I'd been nodding through all this, trying to look newly informed.

Beth went on: "What time is it? I left a message for Albrecht—he was not there when I called—that we would come to the hotel at four o'clock. A nice porter took care of Doris's car for me."

"Lots of time yet." I sipped my coffee. "I was somewhat in the same boat as you, Beth. My parents died when I was a baby."

"Oh, that is sad. And no dear grandmother to bring you up?"

"A dear aunt."

"I'm glad."

"Did you see much of your father before he died?"

"No, I hardly knew him." It was offhand, absent, no evidence of a sense of loss. "His wife wanted him only for herself and her own children."

"How many were there?"

Beth gazed out at Tenth Avenue, reflective and a little bored.

"I think two or three. I saw them only sometimes. One of the girls was at the university with me, but she didn't seem to like me. I think she was jealous. It was true I had many things the other students didn't. My grandmother spoiled me, I admit it. Always she gave me so much, and of course, er dear love too. Now"—her eyes, like Gigi's, went from parkle to fire—"I tell you of Albrecht."

"By all means." I added banally: "Where did you meet ae lucky young man?"

"Well, he is not really very young. He is perhaps twenty ears older than I am. He is being divorced soon."

I shuddered as I thought of Barry's reaction to this. Poor)oris.

Beth sipped her coffee dreamily. "I so wanted to tell all f the nice people I met at Colonel Lockwood's house that ay about Albrecht, but I knew the Colonel was going to nnounce his marriage, and I didn't want to—how can I say —I didn't want to . . ."

"Upstage him?"

Notebook. "Upstage?"

"It means to take attention away from someone."

"Yes, yes." Scribble. "Then Albrecht arrived in New ork day before yesterday by surprise—that is, *as* a surprise r me, and I was so happy and I wanted to ask you if I could ring him to your dinner but he said—he is so—so considrable?"

"Considerate."

"Thank you—and he said no, I must go with Dollfuss as lanned. Again, I wanted to speak of him, but it was an vening for the Colonel and Doris, so I have decided to say othing about Albrecht till they return from their wedding ip."

Oh, good, *good* plan.

Resilience was complete. Beth was studying the dessert 1enu.

"When I go to Frankfurt next week I will tell my grand-10ther. I think she will be pleased. Albrecht is the lawyer r the place of retirement she lives in."

"Why is he in this country?"

"To see me."

You might have figured that one yourself, Clara.

Beth said pridefully: "Albrecht has been wonderful to Jmi—that's a little German pet name for Grandmother. He's

79

been helping her with her business matters since she went into Sonneges Privates Alterscheim. That means—let me think—well, Place of Safe and Sunny Rest. I think I'll have the apple pie.''

11

BETH AND I WALKED EAST ALONG TWENTY-THIRD
Street with all its usual construction and comfortable mixture
of delicatessens, liquor stores, and nice apartment buildings,
and Beth talked about the paragon I was about to meet.

"Albrecht has helped many of the old people at Sonneges
Privates Alterscheim. Some of them cannot handle their
business at all, but Grandmother is not like that. She is very
clear in her mind for eighty-two years of age and quite able
to get around. She allows nobody to wait on her."

I said: "Tell me how to pronounce the name of that place."

As Beth did, I pondered sadly on Karla, who almost fifty
years ago knitted string blankets for her mother and bestowed
her favors on an American officer—wearily? happily? desperately?—whose daughter appeared to have been nondescript and whose granddaughter was brilliant and beautiful.
What fortuitous occurrence of genes had produced Beth? I
wondered.

"Beth, you said your father was a musician. What was his
name?"

"Felix Bauer. He was a violinist." A little laugh. "And I
have no musical talent whatsoever."

"Did you ever know your stepbrothers and sisters?"

"A little, when I was small. But Grandmother seemed to
want not much to do with them. I think she considered herself and myself a little better. I don't want to make her sound
like a—like a—I know this word—snob—but she kept herself
away from them and therefore also me."

I'll bet she did, I thought. Beth and Barry, Barry and Beth, they had been Karla's life, her closely, tenderly, jealously held life, hugged to herself.

We'd arrived at the low-key, rather shabby entrance of the Chelsea Hotel with its proud plaque of names, writers who had lived and labored there. I remembered the day that Henry Gamadge and I, in one of the walks around New York we so loved to take, had stood before the door and read the list:

THOMAS WOLFE
ARTHUR MILLER
DYLAN THOMAS

My eyes misted now before I could read the rest.

We'd gone into the lobby on the strength of that plaque and Henry had said it was hallowed ground. The coffee shop, perhaps less hallowed but very nice, had become one of our favorite places for breakfast.

Now Beth and I walked into the lobby and Beth breathed happily into the phone in German, then turned with word that Albrecht had said to come up.

"Beth, I hope you told him there's somebody with you, somebody who looks like an elderly chaperone." Notebook time. "I mean, did you tell him you're not alone?"

"Of course I did. I said a dear friend was with me and Albrecht must speak English, which he does very well. And I said this friend had been as good to me as if my grandmother, though not yet Umi's great age."

But beginning to feel like it, I thought glumly as we entered the elevator. The prospect of Barry's flood of inquiries about Beth's beloved was already weighing on me. Doris and I must simply gang up on him and tell Barry to mind his own business.

The elevator door opened and a powerfully built man with dark hair and a wide face stood there. He was perhaps forty-five, his clothes were good, if somewhat rumpled, and his hands were outstretched to Beth.

"Elisabeth! And this is your friend."

His English *was* excellent, but there was something wrong

82

with his voice—newly wrong, I gathered, for Beth said quickly: "Albrecht, what is it, what is the matter?"

"Come into the room, *liebling*. Mrs. Gamadge—have I got your name right?—forgive my manners, but I did not trust myself to go down to the lobby."

We walked into the comfortable old room, which was in considerable disarray. Albrecht closed the door and stood with his back to it. He said: "Elisabeth, I am very glad Mrs. Gamadge is with you, for the bad news I have concerns someone you both know." He stepped toward us and stopped. "Dollfuss is dead."

Beth stood as motionless as I. Then I put my arm around her and said: "Sit down."

Albrecht came quickly forward and put her in a chair. I sat on the bed and said: "How?"

Albrecht took Beth's hand. "This is a dreadful thing to tell you. He was—he was almost certainly murdered."

I looked into his white face and said: "Go on."

"He was apparently thrown from the window of his third-floor room into a court early this morning. There had been a struggle. He had been robbed and everything had been taken except a small notebook found in his pocket with a few names and telephone numbers. Yours was one of them, Mrs. Gamadge, and one was mine. In fact, mine was the first, so I received a call first. I have just returned from identifying him."

Beth moved jerkily. "You've seen him?"

"Yes. I went as fast as I could. I was in dread that you would be among the students who had found the body this morning. I asked for you, and someone said you had not returned to your room last night. I was very grateful for that."

Without releasing her hand, Albrecht pulled a chair to Beth's side and sat down. She said: "Did you go up to his room?"

"Yes. The police asked me to search it with them. There was nothing to identify him. Nothing. His passport had also

83

been taken, but that is not a surprise. Passports are very valuable.''

"No mail?" I said. "One—or two—letters?"

Albrecht shook his head. "The police explained that often such things will be swept into a bag to be opened later in search of money. Often when the victim is known to be a traveler. No, the landlady and the other students and myself could alone say that he was Dollfuss Moltke.''

"Which he wasn't," said Beth. She stood up. "Albrecht, may I use your bathroom?''

He rose and put his hand on her elbow. She went past him into the bathroom, closing the door. Albrecht looked at me.

"What does she mean?"

"Mean?"

"That he was not Dollfuss Moltke.''

I removed some strewn clothing from beneath me on the bed. "The Moltke may be genuine, though I doubt it. Only his passport can verify it. But his first name was Adolf. His grandfather was a dedicated Nazi. So was . . . Dollfuss.''

Albrecht stared at me, his eyes steady in his colorless face. Then he drew a breath and sat down again. He said: "In that case, this may have been no routine robbery, no mere struggle with a thief that sent him out of the window. This may have been a ritual slaying.''

"By whom?"

Albrecht leaned forward earnestly. "Mrs. Gamadge, perhaps you do not know that there are fanatical young Nazis among the youth of your country. Here in New York there is an area called Yorkville.''

"I'm familiar with it."

"I know of it because in the course of my law studies I came to this city and learned that Yorkville had been the place of birth of the Nazi party in this country. There could still be fanatical groups dedicated—''

"But Dollfuss himself was fanatically dedicated. Why would his buddies"—did the word sound too flip?—"want to murder him?''

Albrecht shook his head. "You don't understand. Anything—an argument, even an academic one—can set them off. From my childhood I have heard stories . . . ." He looked distractedly past me out of the window. "I could be wrong, of course. Perhaps this was just another robbery and useless killing. But Dollfuss"—his eyes came back to me suddenly—"then the name was—was—"

"Fake." I felt the need to move, to stand up, which I did. "Albrecht—excuse me, I don't know your last name—"

"Pohl. But please, Albrecht."

"Are you absolutely sure the dead man is Dollfuss?"

Albrecht sat up straight. "Mrs. Gamadge, I have seen a few good-looking men in my day, but never one as handsome as this. One could not mistake him."

"His head wasn't damaged, his face not disfigured by the fall?"

"His head, yes. And his neck had been broken. The face, it was discolored, of course. But it was . . . who it was."

The bathroom door had opened. Beth stood there. She said: "I want to look at him."

Brava, Beth.

"Elisabeth!" Albrecht stood up with a shocked expression.

I said: "Albrecht, Beth had reason to be afraid of this young man, a reason connected with what you and I were just talking about. I doubt if she can rest till she knows for herself that he is dead."

He took a step toward her. "Elisabeth, when did you discover that your poor young friend was so tragically committed to—"

"I want to look at him." A monotone.

He shrugged. "Then you shall."

The look she bestowed on him was angelic, if wan, but he missed it in his abstracted stride about the room. He said: "I must find out where they have taken the body. A van came as I was leaving."

I said: "They've taken it to the Medical Examiner on First Avenue behind Bellevue Hospital."

Albrecht looked at me with respect. "Would that be the same as—there's a word, I think begins with an M—"

"Morgue? Yes, much the same."

Beth said quickly: "Clara, come with us!"

"Beth! This is not my—"

"Please. I have no right to ask you but I do. I beg you."

Angelic and wan had given place to stricken and pleading. Albrecht was looking at me with an I-don't-relish-this-either expression.

I said: "Beth, my husband had experience in this end of things—"

"Yes, I have told Albrecht about him and about you."

"—but I have never been inside that place in my life. I don't have a strong stomach, and I could easily pass out and be on your hands."

"No, you won't." Beth took me firmly by the arm. "We're ready, Albrecht."

"Now?" He looked incredulous.

"Right now. We will take Doris's car."

"Take what?" Albrecht's bafflement was complete.

"The car of a friend, which has been loaned to me."

"Elisabeth, I have only just now returned from this *unglück*. I have not even shaved."

"That will only take a few minutes. Clara and I will wait for you in the lobby."

I was dragged from the room and down the hall toward the elevator. I managed to say: "I'll go on one condition, just one."

"What is that?"

"That you let me take Doris's car back to her as soon as we have done this."

"But such a long trip for you!"

"I won't mind."

Then suddenly we faced each other in the elevator.

"Oh, Clara, what do you suppose happened?"

"I don't know. I simply don't know."

We were silent, and the elevator arrived at the lobby. We

walked together to a worn leather sofa and sat on the edge of it.

Beth said: "I heard what Albrecht said about a ritual killing. Do you believe it?"

"No." Nor did I believe it was a routine robbery, unless . . .

"Beth, did Dollfuss carry a lot of money? Do you know if he had much?"

She shook her head. "I think he did not. But of course all the students knew he was traveling and therefore had to have some. Perhaps"—Beth was looking straight ahead—"he was in a fit of being depressed at being shown up as—as—"

"An imposter?"

"Is that someone who is not what he says?" She made a half-hearted gesture toward the notebook, then gave it up. "So he wiped away his identity and destroyed himself."

"But he was proud of his identity. He revealed it himself."

She nodded miserably. I said: "Of course, the passport could have been taken by the first person to find the body. . . . Beth, were you having a love affair?"

"No. He knew about Albrecht from the start. There was never any question of that."

Never any question of that, I thought, looking at her profile. Was that perhaps the cause of "a fit of being depressed"? But Dollfuss had shown no depression last night, nor a sign of anything but elation at the prospect of returning to the homeland.

Perhaps the dead man wasn't Dollfuss after all. Albrecht had probably seen him only a few times. Beth would know instantly, and so, I was pretty sure, would I. Now I was glad I was going.

I had to know too.

12

BUT IT WAS DOLLFUSS.

Beth went quite to pieces. I was amazed at my fortitude as I gazed at the terribly damaged but not wholly destroyed face and the wild, lank, yellow hair. Henry Gamadge would have been proud to see me walk beside the convulsively weeping girl back through the chill, cavernous halls of that warehouse of the dead with Albrecht supporting her and looking freshly devastated himself. Should he fetch the car from the garage we'd put it in and bring it around for us?

I said: "Yes, and take Beth with you, she needs air. So do I, but I also need the bathroom."

He nodded gratefully and went with her out into the sunshine. I was longing for the feel of it myself but I actually needed something else in addition to the bathroom. I walked a short way down the echoing hall and looked into an office that at least had a rug, curtains, and even a plant on the windowsill. An attendant leaned against the wall talking to a girl at a typewriter. They both looked at me as at an apparition. I smiled at the attendant.

"I need some information. Can you help me?"

"I'll try."

"When the police find a dead person, someone who has probably been murdered, what do they do with anything found on the body? Is that brought here too?"

"No, they'd take it back to the precinct. It would be considered evidence."

"Oh. And how would I find out the number and the address of a certain precinct?"

"Call the police, I guess." He looked bored and wandered away. The typist reached for the phone with a good-natured smile.

"Where was the body found?" she asked.

"You're very kind," I said, and told her. Two minutes later I walked out onto First Avenue with a slip of paper in my pocket and a satisfied smile on my face. A horn beeped twice and Albrecht and Beth waved from the car double-parked and idling before the building. I almost wished they'd left it in the garage, so desperate was I for fresh air. I started across the sidewalk toward them and a ghastly memory assailed me. It wasn't raining, there was no old red Buick—only Doris's neat brown Toyota—but as I stepped off the curb Beth's white face told me she had had the same vision, and she buried her face in her hands.

I opened the rear door and said: "Beth and I made a bargain. I get the car."

"Yes." Albrecht looked at Beth's bowed head and said something solicitously in German. She nodded and straightened and looked out of the window. He added: "We passed a filling station where they sell coffee. There we will get a cab."

"I won't abandon you till it comes," I promised as he made a turn.

Albrecht fetched coffee and filled the gas tank, and Beth and I sat gratefully clutching our Styrofoam cups.

She said: "Thank you for everything and for returning the car. Will you tell Colonel Lockwood and Doris about . . ."

"Yes. When do you leave for Germany?"

"Tuesday. That is three days, is it not? Yes, this is Saturday." Beth put her hand to her eyes in a bewildered way that smote me. "I will have two weeks with Umi. I want her not to know of this *unglück*. That means a bad and sad thing. I shall say nothing of it."

"Does she know you're coming?"

"Oh, yes. I think it is not good to have surprises for an old person, even a happy surprise."

"Is Albrecht going with you?"

"Yes. Then he must remain. Perhaps in three or four months his divorce will be settled."

Albrecht opened the back door and handed in the keys with a little bow. "Drive carefully, Mrs. Gamadge. Elisabeth will go back to the hotel with me. Tomorrow we will look for another room for her near the university. I wish her not to return to that unhappy place."

There was no question he was caring and capable, but I felt an overwhelming reluctance to leave the girl. I got out of the back of the car and into the driver's seat. Beth leaned over and kissed me.

I said: "Wait a minute. I said I'd stay here till you got a cab."

"I think we do," said Beth and got out of the car. Sure enough, Albrecht was flagging one to the curb. He came and took Beth's arm and said: "Safe trip."

"Thanks for the gas and the coffee," I replied lamely and they waved as I pulled into the street.

I drove straight up First Avenue and found a parking lot two blocks from precinct headquarters on One hundred twenty-sixth Street. I walked the two blocks gratefully, breathing in the tainted air that actually seemed to have a freshness to it, or was I just relieved to be alone and walking? It was after five and smoggy twilight was upon the city. My reception at the somber old precinct building was polite but bewildered. What was this white-haired, tweedy old dame who said things like "I would *so* appreciate your help" doing here at this hour? I was finally relegated to a room with a youngish, pimply, slope-shouldered officer who exactly fitted my image of a favorite Dickens character, Dick Swiveller.

"I do hope you can give me some information, officer."

"Sure, ma'am"—staring.

"Last night—no, early this morning—a young man was found dead on Morningside Drive—"

"Yeah, yeah, some German guy. No identification."

"I understand there was a notebook on the body with some names and addresses."

"Yeah, one was another German name. The guy came."

"And the name Gamadge was in it. That's me."

Interest was born. "You knew him?"

"Yes, but not well. I'd just met the poor boy. Would it be possible to see the notebook?"

Dick Swiveller rose and walked to the door smiling over his shoulder. "You sound like my Mom. She'd call him 'a poor boy' too, The guy was no kid."

"He was to your Mom and me."

He returned presently with a file from which he took a small, almost new spiral notebook. He handed it to me.

There on the first page were Albrecht's name and phone number. Bud's Pizza and number were on the second page and mine on the third with Friday's date and 7 P.M., the little foreign stroke across the 7. That was all. But Dollfuss had had other acquaintances: Anna and Barry for two. Why were their names not in the book? I turned back and studied the spiral.

When you tear a page from these notebooks it usually leaves a fringe, a jagged fragment dangling from the spiral. There were several dangling fragments.

I said: "Is it pretty certain he was murdered?"

"Oh, sure. Cleaned out first."

"Will there be—will you investigate?"

Shrug. "Nothing to go on."

I said thank you and handed the notebook back to Dick Swiveller. The great white-faced clock on the wall said 6:10 and I knew the street would be almost dark. Remembering the days when my husband and I had strolled Manhattan at all hours, I hated the feeling of needing to hurry back to the parking lot. Grow up, Clara, I said, and got into the car and locked the door.

A certain contentment settled on me as I jounced my way out of the city. I enjoyed driving; in fact, missed our car, which I'd let go when Henry died. On the Saw Mill River Parkway I realized it would be nine or ten o'clock before I reached Connecticut and decided not to stop. I reached into the backseat for the doggy bag, extracted the soggy tuna fish sandwich and munched on it. This took my thoughts back to the diner and to Beth's cavalier dismissal of her father and his second family. There was a haze over the picture, not a healthy one.

Had Karla's possessiveness been fair to Beth? Surely there ought to have been more contact with her father before "he drank" and "he died." And a growing-up acquaintance with her stepbrothers and -sisters might have been wholesome for the solitary child. The stepsister at the university had been jealous. Figured. Accounts of the air of privilege that surrounded the golden Elisabeth must have gone home, and one could imagine the speculation and resentment. The girl's grandmother had been, after all, only married to a farmer. How had Karla acquired the Purse of Fortunatus? Envy and curiosity can be a deadly combination . . . The haze over the picture deepened, and by the time I reached Lake Winifred, glimmering palely, my thoughts were as dark as the sky.

I slowed as I approached The Chapel in the Elms. The hall alongside it, connected by a breezeway to the chapel, was bright with lights, and figures moved about inside. The clock in the car said nine-fifteen. I drove a short way to a vaguely designated corner with a granite marker and turned right. Barry's cottage appeared, a light over the front door. What I assumed was Doris's house, an old-fashioned framed edifice beside it, was dark.

I turned into Doris's driveway and my lights swept Barry's windows. He looked out of one of them, then emerged from the front door and came hurrying across the grass.

He called: "Beth?"

I opened the door and the dome light revealed me. I said: "Clara."

He almost stumbled. "Clara—my God—what in the world—"

"I'd like a drink, please."

"Of course, but what—"

"Where's Doris?"

"At the chapel."

"Good. Shall I put the car in the garage?"

92

"No, leave it there. You shouldn't have done this, Clara. We'd have fetched it. Give me the keys."

I unbuckled my seat belt and climbed stiffly out. Barry, in tee-shirt and baggy chinos, looked more informal than I'd ever seen him. He put his arm around me and we walked across the totally dark grass toward his house. A pure white, scampering kitten materialized beside me and I scooped it up. Barry said it was Doris's and that she was a cat lover.

"Me too," I said. I tried to hold onto the ball of fluff but it struggled down and away. "What's going on at the chapel?"

"They're getting ready for the senior citizens tomorrow. A Mother's Day dinner."

Mother's Day. Was that "arbitrary festival," as Sadd called it, upon us again? Flowers and candy and mothers; frozen corpses and morgues. Did young Adolf Whatever-his-name-was have a living mother, she of the picture he carried? Would she ever learn his fate?

We walked into Barry's living room and he snapped off the television and put me on the sofa.

"Bourbon?"

"Please. But get me your briefcase first."

He stopped en route to his bar and looked at me. "Briefcase?"

"Have you looked in it since last night?"

"No. I only drag it out to work with Beth."

"Get it for me."

"It's in front of you on the shelf under the coffee table. Am I to understand that on the strength of what I read last night you plan to recommend me for the Pulitzer—"

"Oh, be quiet." I was riffling through the briefcase. There it was. I pulled the photograph out and, forcing myself to be patient, put it faceup on the coffee table. Barry came back with my drink and stared down.

"Where did that come from?"

"From your briefcase. Beth put it there last night."

He seemed incapable of motion. I had to reach out and take the glass from him.

I said: "Barry, sit down."

He did, beside me, not taking his eyes from my face. I began with the return visit of Dollfuss after the party; I reported my conversation with Beth at lunch; I got carefully through "meeting a friend of Beth's from Germany," and, knowing how Albrecht must have felt as he uttered them, I came to the words "Dollfuss is dead." I wound up with our identification of the robbed and murdered man.

"That is," I added, "our identification of him as Dollfuss Moltke."

Barry hadn't moved. Now I gathered my courage and picked up the photograph. I said: "You told me your daughter's husband remarried after she died."

"Yes."

"And his second wife was a widow with children of her own."

"Yes."

"Do you remember her name—her first married name?"

"Ritter. Karla used to mention her. She didn't like her."

I took a last look at the quartet in the photograph. Attractive young lieutenant and Mrs. Barry Lockwood, and behind them the two members of Hitler's elite SS, one handsome, the other toadlike.

I turned the picture over and held it between us.

Some penciled writing and a faded ink stamp. The stamp, in the upper left corner, read:

> Johann Steimmetz, Photographie
> 2088 Wilmantstrasse
> Munchen

Then in pencil: DREI ABZÜGE.

"What does that mean?" I asked.

Barry cleared his throat. "Three copies."

Three names and addresses followed, but I was no more capable of reading them aloud than was Barry. We simply sat and stared at them.

First Lieutenant Barry Lockwood
118th Inf. Bn.
23rd Inf. Div.
Fort Devens, Massachusetts, U.S.A.

Ober Leutnant Ernst Ritter der Schutzpolizie
Reichsführung—SS
Berlin SW11

Reichsführer SS Heinrich Himmler
Reichsführung—SS
Berlin SW11

The horror of the third name rendered the revelation of
the second almost anticlimactic.

Barry moved stiffly. He took the photograph and shied it
across the room. It lay, a gray patch on the carpet. His voice
was harsh.

"It would seem the young man in the morgue is Adolf
Ritter. Beth's stepbrother."

Now for the crunch.

I said: "Barry, was he blackmailing you?"

13

BARRY SAT STILL FOR A FEW SECONDS, THEN HE stood up and held out his hand for my glass.

"Refill?"

"No, thanks."

He walked away a few steps, then came back. He said: "Where's Beth? Is she okay?"

"She's okay. She's with her . . . her friend from Germany."

"Is she still going back there?" I nodded. "Does Karla know she's coming?"

"Yes. Barry, I asked you a question."

"I haven't heard from Karla in a while." He walked about aimlessly. "I'd better send her money for Beth's trip."

I thought of the apparently well-off Albrecht and his enveloping solicitude. "Beth said nothing about needing money. You've got to quit this Masked Protector routine, Barry. The girl is going to live her own life. Repeat: were you being blackmailed?"

He sighed and sat down again.

"Not exactly 'being' blackmailed. It was a one-shot, amateur sort of thing. He phoned the day before your party to say that he knew Beth was my granddaughter—backed up the statement with lots of names, dates, and places—and if I didn't want him making an ugly scene at your dinner, I was to bring twenty thousand dollars. He said I had to agree it wasn't much for a 'wealthy' man like me—ha!—and he'd leave the country the next day and I'd never hear from him again, et cetera, et cetera. So, of course, I brought the cash and gave it to him. During dessert, appropriately.''

I could only gasp, like the mayor's daughter in *The Music Man*: "Ye gods!"

Barry grunted. "Well, he got mugged and murdered for his pains. What a haul for the thief. You'd almost think . . ." He looked at me. "Do you suppose some of his Nazi pals were in on the scam?"

I shrugged and Barry got up again. "What bothered me most was his knowing about Beth. Of course, now that we know he was a Ritter . . . But how did he get to Karla? She had to be his source. Not that she'd spill anything on purpose—she'd rather die—but she's in her eighties. God knows what I may be babbling at that point."

I looked with compassion at his haggard face. "It's too awful, Barry, having your money go like that."

"It could be worse." Barry walked away a few steps, then stood still. "At least I saved Beth from being kicked in the face by a stranger. And it was a reasonable gamble. Well, fairly reasonable."

"Gamble?" I was uncomprehending.

He looked down at the picture, touched it with his foot, then glanced sideways at me with the ghost of a smile.

"You don't think I planned to let that blond bandit *keep* the money, do you?"

Still uncomprehending, but with a sudden thumping in my chest, I sat still. Barry went on:

"I had a few adventures myself last night."

I said nothing.

"I just wanted to hear yours first."

I said: "I may kill you."

His short laugh brought a touch of color back to Barry's face. He pulled a straight chair forward and sat down facing me.

"When we left your place we all stood on the sidewalk talking for a few minutes. I was playing for time—I wanted to pry Beth loose from the guy. Finally Henry and Tina took off, and I suggested that Beth come home with us to work

97

on the book over the weekend. Much to my relief, she seemed anxious to come. Dollfuss—I guess we're stuck with the name—was ticked at first, then he was suddenly all for it—we know now it gave him a chance to go back for his picture—and he said good night and marched off. Walking to the garage to get our car I was trying to figure his time: how long would it be till he got back to his digs on Morningside Drive, and then would he take off right away?—that was my dread. I didn't know he was giving me a break by going back to pay you a visit.''

Barry hadn't taken his eyes from my face, but now he folded his hands on his crossed knees and looked down at them.

''I drove as far as Riverdale because I wanted the car out of the city for Doris, then I suddenly went into a head-slapping routine and 'remembered' an appointment with my lawyer in Manhattan this morning. The girls should keep on going to Lake Winifred and I'd catch a cab to a hotel. Doris started to say they'd stay in with me, but then—thank God!—she remembered this Mother's Day thing, and I told Beth I'd be back this afternoon to work with her. I pointed them in the right direction and caught a cab—to Morningside Drive. Oh, I meant to mention something else.'' Barry looked back at me. ''I had my .45 automatic that I haven't touched since Korea.''

Terrible thumping in my chest now, but an inner voice that kept saying there was no bullet hole, there was no bullet hole, there was no—

''Clara, honey!'' Barry looked alarmed. He reached over and grabbed my hand. ''I didn't kill him. All I was going to do was hold him up for my own money and then go home and level with Beth. When I got to his place he was lying dead in the court with a crowd around him. Just listening I learned he'd been robbed as well.'' Barry released my hand and stood up. ''And I'd lost my gamble.''

He put his chair back in its place and looked down at the picture again. ''I spent the rest of the night in a fleabag in the area. I called you from there and felt like a bum when I woke you up and I decided it would all keep. When I got home, Doris came over to say Beth had left, but that was okay, she was safe now. I told Doris where I'd been and what I'd done and why. Do you know what she said?'' Barry looked at me in loving wonderment. ''She said she thought she'd have done the same thing. And then she went over to get ready for the senior citizens.''

Great admiration kept me silent.

Barry leaned down and picked up the picture. He said, tearing it to bits: ''I know you're right, Clara. I should lay off. Beth doesn't need me.''

Great pity kept me silent.

''I think . . .'' Barry looked over my head at nothing. ''I want her to know, at some point, but I want it to be me or Karla who tells her.''

''I buy that.''

He started toward the kitchen. ''Are you hungry? I don't have much. I usually eat at Doris's. I think there's peanut butter.''

''I'll make a sandwich.'' My third of the day.

Barry sat on a breakfast stool and watched me spread peanut butter.

''Clara, why was Anna murdered?''

I cut the sandwich in half and took a bite. Everybody knows that peanut butter has a way of locking the jaws. I signaled as much to Barry, and he went to the refrigerator and poured a glass of milk. This bought me just enough time to decide not to say: Barry, do you remember the letter, the fat letter with the German stamps, fat perhaps with names, dates, places . . . a letter that would have sent Anna flying to confront you with your sins—worse—confront Beth with them, thereby spoiling a blackmail scheme? Of course we can't know this for certain, Barry, because the letter is gone and Adolf Ritter is gone . . .

Why torture the man with bitter and useless speculation on the eve of a happy new life? I took a swallow of milk and

99

said with utter truthfulness: "I wish I knew, Barry. I sure wish I knew."

The back door opened and Doris came in breathlessly.

"Clara, you shouldn't have done it, but I'm grateful because we'll need cars tomorrow. Some of the real old-timers—" she looked from me to Barry.

"Barry, you told her about Dollfuss."

"She already knew, dear. And Beth knows."

Doris looked distressed. "How—"

"Doris," I said firmly, "we're not going to talk about it. It's over. At some point, maybe after your honeymoon, I'll give you my version. Now, what can I do to help?"

"Open the cabinet behind you and give me those paper plates." Then, as I did so: "I do hope Beth is still going to Germany to visit her grandmother."

"She is."

"The change will do her good. Poor girl. What an ordeal."

Doris clucked on, but she was very happy, and like most people in that blessed state she was finding it hard to react to tragedy once removed. She sorted spoons. "It all began with that darned picture, didn't it? I don't imagine either of you will ever want to look at it again. You should throw it away."

Barry started, then looked down at his clenched right fist. From it still protruded the shiny scraps. Doris gently loosened his fingers and held his hand over the trash basket. Then she kissed him and said: "Clara, I wish you'd stay for our Mother's Day dinner tomorrow."

"I'd love to, if I can help."

"You can. You can pick up a couple of mothers."

It was good to hear Barry burst out laughing, though to this day I don't know why.

As I waved Barry off late the next afternoon and opened my storm door, I stumbled over an enormous bouquet wedged inside. A note in my son's handwriting read:

100

We know you'd prefer murder for Mother's Day but this was the best we could do. Where the hell have you been? We came to take you to dinner. Call us.

I went upstairs and did so, grateful for the distraction. I'd been trying to thrust from my mind a disturbing thought that had lodged there in the course of the wakeful night at Doris's and had nagged me during the drive home.

Tina and Henry, on their respective extensions, listened in horrified silence to my account of yesterday's drama. This time I included Albrecht in the cast of characters, but omitted mention of the sordid shakedown and loss that Barry had suffered. I was haunted and depressed by it and felt his privacy should be respected. I did, however, part with another confidence when my son, with all his father's insidious sense of something held back, said: "I don't get it, Mom. Why is this Beth girl looming so large in Barry Lockwood's life? There's a piece of this puzzle missing, and I'll bet you're sitting on it."

I admitted I was, and told them. They were entitled.

"Does Doris know?" asked Tina.

"Yes."

Henry said impatiently: "Why doesn't Barry just tell the girl? She'd probably be thrilled to know he's her grandfather."

I said some trite things about how the roots of old secrets go deep, how there was another person to be considered, namely Beth's grandmother, how they must remember it happened in an era less tolerant than this one—

"Adolf." Henry was off on another tack. "What a name. Sinister even now. And he was Beth's stepbrother. That's a relationship she *won't* be thrilled with. Does she know?"

"Not yet."

"Who gets to tell her the lovely fact?"

"Not I, Henry."

Tina said, "I'm glad she has this Albrecht guy, at least. You said he seems to adore her."

"Yes."

"Funny about that mugging." Henry was not his father's son for nothing. "Was it the Nazi connection, do you think?"

"Who knows?"

Tina said, "Is Beth still going to Germany to visit Grandma?"

"Day after tomorrow."

"Then we can get the newlyweds off to Greece before any more horrendous disclosures?"

"I sure hope so," I said wearily.

Henry said, "Take a nap, Mom. You've earned it."

I may have earned it but I couldn't collect. I sat in the wing chair by the fireplace, grateful for the solitude at least. Coiled in my mind lay Disturbing Thought. I kept saying to myself that it was truly no longer any of my business. Let me think of something that was: tomorrow was Monday, bridge day (had all this taken place within one week?). I'd call Sara and we'd decide on a fourth to take Anna's place. Anna. Oh, Anna, poor, poor you. I'd been dozing, and now I found myself awake and weeping as the phone rang.

It was Beth. I felt instant irritation. This gorgeous creature had disrupted my life for one entire week and I was sick of it. Disturbing Thought could go jump in the lake.

"Beth, I'm really awfully tired—"

"Clara! My grandmother is arriving at Kennedy Airport in two hours!"

Wait a minute. "I thought you—"

"Yes, but she and Albrecht decided to surprise me!" Her voice vibrated like a tuning fork. "Isn't it wonderful? She's always wanted to visit America. Albrecht has rented a car and we're just leaving for the airport. Now I have a favor to ask."

Oh, God.

"And I will never, never ask another for I have asked you too much already but here is the favor: may I bring Umi to stay with you for one night—for one night only? There is no opening at the Chelsea till tomorrow, then we can settle her here. I will tell her all about you. I know she will be anxious to meet you!"

Like fun she will, I thought exhaustedly. The poor old lady had probably been shoved on a plane through the officiousness of Albrecht trying to make Brownie points with her granddaughter. How old was Karla? Eighty-odd. Was she up to this? Then I recalled that Edith Hamilton had made four trips to Europe after her ninetieth birthday. Maybe Karla was a gutsy old frau only too anxious for a spree. Meanwhile Beth was saying she knew this was a terrible imposition, et cetera. Well, I was back in the mare's nest with a vengeance, so I might as well go whole hog and let Disturbing Thought surface again.

"Of course she can come, Beth. I'd love to meet your grandmother. But I have a favor to ask in return."

"Anything, anything! What is it?"

"I'll tell you when you get here."

I ran a tub and sank into it, musing on the obtuseness of the young. After yesterday, a house guest was the last thing I wanted. I longed to do just one thing: go to bed and stay there till morning. How long did I have? It was going on five now. The plane was due in two hours, which probably meant three, then customs, then another hour or more back to Manhattan; it could be nine or ten o'clock. I reached for my robe feeling cheered already.

Now the only problem was going to be how to prevent Beth from suggesting merrily that Umi be included in Barry's wedding festivities. "Colonel, I want you to meet my dear grandmother." A vision of Barry and Karla solemnly shaking hands nearly did me in as I turned back my bedspread. What could be arranged for Karla that day? The Statue of Liberty? Giggling weakly, I was in bed, then gradually sick at heart as Disturbing Thought enveloped me like a fog.

14

THEY ARRIVED ABOUT NINE-THIRTY.

I saw the car from the window I'd taught myself to look out of without dread. Albrecht assisted a tiny, white-haired woman in a black coat from the backseat. Beth followed, the trunk yielded a small bag, and Albrecht pulled away again, presumably to park. I walked to my admittance buzzer and pressed it. Standing there waiting for the elevator, I told Disturbing Thought that this was not the moment.

My front door opened and Beth flew out and embraced me. She towered over the little woman behind her as she drew her forward.

"Clara, this is my dear grandmother, Mrs. Spenhoff."

Maria Ouspenskaya. Remember the little Russian actress who played all the elegant, foreign old ladies in the forties movies?

"Mrs. Gamadge, Elisabeth has told me so much about you."

Yep, same picaresque accent.

I said: "Mrs. Spenhoff, I feel as if I know you already." The eerie element of truth in the remark struck me as I took their coats and we sat down. I dutifully asked about the flight. It had been long. We agreed on that for a while and then I said I had been to Germany but was not familiar with Prenzlau and where was it? It was in the north. Mr. Spenhoff had been a farmer and most of Germany's best farmland was in the north. I recalled that I had once sailed from Bremerhaven, was that not in the north? It was. Beth said that one of her favorite childhood stories had been "The Musicians of

Bremen," about the four animals—why, of course, one of mine too, and I had often read it to my own children, and by now I felt like a victrola running sluggishly to a stop.

"Can I get you something to eat?" The saving question.

Thank you, but Umi had had dinner on the plane and Beth wanted nothing. Then Umi requested the bathroom and Beth took her to it as the buzzer sounded. I admitted Albrecht. His look was decidedly sheepish and he said at once: "It was a very sudden decision. I was most anxious to surprise Elisabeth."

"And you did."

"Mrs. Spenhoff has wanted to come to this country ever since Elisabeth did. It could be her last opportunity. She is quite frail, as you can see."

"Oh, I don't know. She looks amazingly fit."

"She is. She is indeed. When she first entered Sonneges Privates Alterscheim—that is the place of retirement for which I am legal—"

"Yes, Beth told me."

"When she first came there she was rather—rather confused, but she adjusted very well and is now as clear in her head as a person ten years younger."

I'm a person ten years younger, I thought, and I'm not too clear in my head right now.

I said: "Does she have any friends or relatives who visit her at the home?"

"Not that I know of. I believe she is very much alone."

"Can I get you a drink, Albrecht?"

"Thank you, no. We are most grateful for your hospitality tonight. I wanted another hotel but Elisabeth begged for this. Tomorrow we will come for the lady, perhaps in the later morning. I want very much to go early with Elisabeth to look for another student room."

"When will you return to Germany?"

"I will wait for the grandmother now. Perhaps a few weeks."

The man must be made of money. Flights sacrificed, others effected overnight, job on hold.

Beth and Karla appeared.

Beth said: "Clara, you said on the phone you had a favor to ask. What is it?"

She was too happy. And Disturbing Thought could hardly be verbalized in the presence of Albrecht and Umi.

"No hurry, Beth. You and Albrecht go along and I'll get your grandmother to bed." I turned to her with a sympathetic smile. "If you're anything like me, jet lag lays you low."

The poor woman looked bewildered, and we laughed. Beth hugged her. "Not only does she not know what jet lag is, she has never been across the ocean before. Are you tired, Umi?"

"A little."

Smart lady to admit it and save us an evening of innocuous conversation.

Beth and Albrecht departed and I turned from the front door, longing for bed. I walked to the wing chair where Karla sat and held out my hands to her.

"If you're sure you don't want anything to eat, let me tuck you in. We can talk in the morning."

She smiled up at me—she'd been pretty once, you can always tell—and gave me her hands. "Perhaps just a glass of milk?"

I nodded. "Your room is right in here."

She followed me to the guest bedroom and said: "What pretty wallpaper."

"I hope the traffic sounds don't keep you awake. We city dwellers are used to them. On your farm—"

"In Frankfurt my room is over a busy street also."

A heck of a good guest, I thought gratefully as I went to the kitchen. The kind who's already eaten, wants to go to bed at a reasonable hour, and doesn't mind traffic sounds. And she'll sleep late, and by the time we've had breakfast we'll barely have scratched the surface of banalities about grandchildren before she's fetched.

When I returned with the milk, Karla was sitting on the bed in a blue robe, brushing her short, nicely groomed hair.

She said: "My mother had beautiful long white hair like yours and wore it the way you do."

"Sometimes I feel like a dinosaur," I said. "But my husband would never let me cut it, and now my daughter begs me not to."

"Then you must not."

"Can I get you anything else, Mrs. Spenhoff?"

"No, thank you. And please call me Karla."

"All right. And my name is rather like yours. It's Clara."

"So Barry told me."

It's probably a good thing I had my hand on the bedpost or I might have done what my son calls "take a dive." She'd said it quietly, not looking at me. Now she put her hairbrush on the bedside table and turned with brimming eyes.

"How is he?"

"Very well. Very happy. He's getting married this week."

"Yes, he told me. I'm so pleased for him."

Karla took off her robe and got her tiny frame into the bed. I snapped out the light beside her and started toward the door.

Her voice came to me, quivering but distinct: "Thank you for being so good to our granddaughter."

Bravo, Henry, you did not lose it nearly so well, I'd have
rattled my ... and words were piled. Captain Ed-
mond, who had sat ... on to ... winceable fire, said: "Go

15

THE NEXT AFTERNOON SARA AND EVE AND I SAT
looking across my bridge table in awe at the diminutive figure
making short work of Sara's trumps. Karla's little hands flew
as she gathered in the tricks.

"Anna would love her," murmured Sara, and the irony
of the remark struck me. "Quite a fourth you found for us,
Clara."

Karla said: "I have always loved cards. Many years ago I
learned bridge from some of your American servicemen.
Then I became out of practice. But since going to the retirement home I have played every day."

"I believe it," said Eve, gazing at the score pad.

We played in respectful silence.

Karla and I had awakened almost simultaneously that
morning. It was a chilly one, and I made a fire and we sat
before it rather like rediscovered old friends, gossiping and
sipping coffee.

"Does Beth look like her mother?" I asked.

"She has Louise's gray eyes but that is all. When she was
a little girl I would send pictures and Barry would write 'I
think she looks like you,' but I was never beautiful."

"Does she have any of her father's qualities?"

"No, all of her grandfather's!" It was a paean.

"What do you think of Albrecht?"

Her face changed. "I wish there was not in his life so
much confusions—no, there's a better word—"

"Complications?"

"That is it. He has children. He has a wife who is making

the divorce difficult. Of course, he is brilliant and charming.''

"And Beth is dazzled."

"I'm afraid so."

We sat in silence for a moment. Karla suddenly leaned forward as if to speak, then only reached for the cream pitcher.

I said: "Tell me about your daughter."

"Louise was very gentle." Karla's voice was very gentle too. "She was shy, not sharp like Elisabeth. When she married Felix I was pleased, and Barry sent money for a lovely wedding. But poor Felix drank and Louise was not strong. At Elisabeth's birth there was a crisis. Louise told me it was the baby who must live."

I apologized mentally to Louise for having thought her nondescript.

I said: "Beth said you didn't keep in touch with her father's second family."

"No. His new wife was dedicated to the memory of the Third Reich. Also she was very jealous of Beth. She had children of her own."

"Did you ever see the children?"

"Once or twice. I think it was two girls and a boy. The little boy was very handsome, I recall. But it has not been for years."

Not for years. Then how had Dollfuss/Adolf learned . . . and would Karla have known him if she saw him? Had all of the family come upon her past? I looked at the contented little figure holding her feet to the fire and hated myself for my next thought: Was Karla herself to be trusted? With Barry's approaching marriage, had she been fearful for her source of supply? Disturbing Thought took on a nasty new dimension.

She said suddenly: "Tell me about the woman Barry will marry. Do you like her?"

"Very much."

"I am glad." Karla put her cup on the table between us. "He deserves happiness after these long years, and the years before that with the so jealous lady, what was her name—Anna. Is she still living?''

I watched Karla's face. ''She was killed last week.''

''Killed!'' Karla's startled reaction certainly seemed like the genuine article.

''She was run over in a traffic accident.''

I was spreading butter on toast. I extended the plate to Karla and looked into her eyes. They met mine in dismay.

''Oh, the poor soul, the poor soul!''

I guess I was convinced. I sat back and said: ''How long ago did your husband die?''

''Oh, many years.'' Karla seemed to rouse herself. ''He was a kind man and fond of Louise even though he too had children of his own.''

Stepbrothers and -sisters coming out of the woodwork! How had Karla maintained her cover this long? I wondered.

The phone had rung at that moment. It was Eve inquiring if I'd gotten a fourth. Karla said she couldn't help overhearing my end of the conversation and modestly offered to fill in. I accepted out of courtesy, and we'd called Beth to ask if my visitor might stay till evening. I took Karla as my partner in case she proved an embarrassment, which she did, though not in the way I'd expected. I myself played wretchedly, Disturbing Thought demanding I do something at once. But how?

Oddly, it was Sadd who provided the wedge.

Albrecht and Beth arrived at five. The game broke up and we sat with drinks, Beth smiling proudly at the compliments heaped on her grandmother.

Eve said: ''She's an even better player than Anna, and that's saying something.''

Beth looked a little daunted. ''Yes—I remember Anna loved playing bridge. She was a friend of ours, Umi. She—She died last week.''

Karla nodded, her eyes on her granddaughter's face.

Albrecht said lightly: ''The world cannot afford to lose a good bridge player.''

''Albrecht is himself a fine player.'' This from Karla.

Beth looked surprised. "I didn't know."

Albrecht smiled modestly. "You will have to put up with my middle-aged hobbies, *liebling*. Or perhaps it will be one of my pleasures to teach you the game."

Sara and Eve looked politely inquiring, and I asked if it would be telling tales out of school to say Albrecht and Beth hoped to be married. It would not, and there were smiles and congratulations. Beth took out her notebook to record "tales out of school."

"Albrecht," Karla put her head back in the depths of the wing chair, "do you remember the day I came to the Alterscheim, and how because of your kindness, a bridge game made me feel at home?"

"Now, Karla, it was not my kindness at all. You were—"

"Yes, it was and I want to tell everyone." She became animated, sitting forward. "I was in my room and everything I owned was piled in boxes and I was so tired and looking for a place to lie down. Albrecht came in to ask for a copy of my will, which must be placed in the safe in the office, and I said I was too tired to look for it and he said he would help me. We started to go through things and he found my playing cards and some old tallies. We discovered that we both enjoyed bridge, and Albrecht said there was a game in progress in the common room at that moment and he would take me down and introduce me and I could play and forget my tiredness. He was right, and when I returned to my room Albrecht had put all my things in order. I shall never forget that kindness."

"Was I not a saintly character?" Albrecht rose as the phone rang.

I was sitting next to the desk and able to reach the receiver without getting up. It was Sadd, calling from Kennedy, to announce that he had fled from the Toronto madhouse his daughter called home. I told him I had guests and would take the call in the kitchen. I said: "Sal, hang up when you know I'm on," and made my way out of the room aware that they were all rising to go.

111

In the kitchen I said: "Sadd, listen to me—"

"Don't preach. You'd have left too. Those children are savages."

"That isn't what I was—"

"And illiterate. Totally illiterate. The television is never off and neither of them can read or write, at the age of nine."

"That's a ridiculous exaggeration, and if you'll just let me—"

"In addition there are two monstrous dogs who leap all over you, slobber, shed hair—Clara, I'm taking a cab. Can you put me up? I promise—"

"How would you like somebody to come for you?"

"Are you insane? I wouldn't dream of letting you—"

"Shut up and listen to me." I began to talk, dropping my voice and looking anxiously toward the door. Sadd kept saying "What? What? Speak up, woman." I spoke up as loud as I dared.

Finally he said: "Well, all right, but this has all the earmarks of one of your seizures. What's this character's name . . . ? He's Beth's *what* . . . ? I hate him already. I'm to look exhausted and sick? That's absolutely no problem. Tell him I'll be in a bar just off the baggage turntable of Canadian Airlines. It's called Cloud's End. Actually, the apostrophe is in the wrong place. 'Clouds' should be taken as plural—"

I hung up and returned to the others with a distressed look. Beth said at once: "Clara, what is it?"

"It's Sadd. He had to come back early from Toronto. He's sick. Albrecht, I have a tremendous favor to ask: this is an elderly gentleman, a cousin of mine. Could you possibly pick him up at Kennedy? I know this is a dreadful imposition . . ."

I jabbered on, looking everywhere but into the eyes of Albrecht, which were, I'm sure, filled with indignation. Two trips to Kennedy in two days! But he was trapped. Kind Mrs. Gamadge had been so good to Beth and Karla, who were now looking at him expectantly. I had an instant's flash of fear that Beth would offer to go with him and ended my plea hastily with the words: "I'll see that the ladies get safely back to the hotel."

I gave the glowering Albrecht a description of Sadd and the location of Cloud's End, and he departed with as good grace as he could muster. Sara and Eve followed him down and I closed the door and took a deep breath, feeling a little sick.

Beth and Karla were looking at ornaments and family pictures about the room and chatting in German.

I said: "If we walk to the corner of Madison we're more likely to get a cab."

"Clara," said Beth, "you don't have to—"

"I'm going to the hotel with you."

They both protested and continued to protest all the way down in the elevator and out the front door, but I trudged with my executioner's step beside them, saying I always welcomed a chance to visit the Chelsea. Mercifully, a cab materialized and my companions were too busy pointing out the window and craning and explaining to notice my abstraction. We alighted at the Chelsea and I grossly overtipped the driver in my haste to beat Beth to the fare and get us inside the hotel.

As Karla registered I said quietly to Beth: "I'll wait here. Get your grandmother settled in her room and come back. It's important."

She looked startled but nodded and they went up. I sat miserably on the edge of the same sofa we'd sat miserably on the edge of the day before. The cheerful bustle of the lobby might have been the howl of demons, so leaden was my heart. Beth was back in ten minutes and sat beside me.

I said rapidly: "Beth, I'm going to ask you to do something very hard. If it turns out as I think, we'll have to move fast. If I'm wrong you need never speak to me again."

She sat like a statue.

"Say nothing to your grandmother. Go up to Albrecht's

room and search it thoroughly. Examine everything, especially the linings of things. I believe you'll find Dollfuss's passport and twenty thousand dollars in American money."

16

I STOOD LOOKING AT KARLA AND BETH, WHO were huddled on the bed together, drowning in horror. The thing lay beside them like an ugly green blot, and next to it a long brown envelope with the cash.

Karla rocked the hysterical Beth and kept repeating: "It's my fault, my fault, my fault! Why did I let you come without knowing? Why didn't I tell you? Why didn't *Barry* tell you?"

Damn right, Karla, why didn't he? But we've been all through that and it's too late and now we're at Albrecht's mercy.

"Put it all back!" gasped Beth. "Then he won't know we know!"

She reached wildly for the hateful objects but I seized her hand.

"Not on your life!" Every hackle I possessed rose. "That's your grandfather's money and he's going to get it back. He gave it to Dollfuss, and Albrecht took it from Dollfuss and killed him."

"No!" It was a shriek.

"Beth, listen to me: they were in this together and Dollfuss was the legman. Albrecht fed him the stuff he found in your grandmother's correspondence—am I right, Karla?"

The poor soul nodded weakly.

"But instead of sharing it, Dollfuss was going to vamoose."

"Why do you keep saying 'Dollfuss'?" Beth sat up wild-eyed. "Why don't you say Adolf Ritter, my almost bruzzer, who Albrecht so kindly found for me, so *kindly found*—"

"Stop it, Beth." Practical severity was in order here. "Think how much you meant to Barry that he should do what he did rather than have you hurt."

With a moan the girl sank into her grandmother's arms again. I looked around for a chair—I hadn't sat down in a while—but stood up straight with Karla's next, quiet words.

"And I have done the same."

Beth's head came up with a jerk and mine did something similar.

Karla went on, still rocking: "Oh, yes, I've been giving Albrecht money ever since you came to this country. Why do you think I am here? Because he brought me? That is what he told you. It was I who said I was coming, and he was furious. I have been in such fear for you, Elisabeth. He said if I exposed him . . . and his terrible need for money . . . How could I let you stay here with him? But how could I let you come back to Germany, back where I have no friends because I am so old?" The rocking accelerated. "I decided to come to *your* friends with my fright and trouble, and now"—her voice broke—"I have caused *them* fright and trouble."

I said, looking at my watch in considerable fright and trouble: "Karla, why didn't you tell me all this at my place this morning? It would have saved—"

"Oh, I came so close, so close!" She stroked the bright head of her granddaughter, who now lay inert in her arms. "But I did not want to pull Barry into it because he has been so good to me. I said to myself I will wait a few days until he is married and gone away and then I will ask Mrs. Gamadge who helps people and has been so kind—"

Much more kindness from me, I thought, and we're all dead. Karla's voice took on a pleading note.

"I did try to let you know a little when I told about the bridge game and how Albrecht had stayed in my room, for I keep all of Barry's letters—"

Yes, I'll give you that, Karla. Disturbing Thought had crystalized into Terrible Certainty at that moment. And the letter . . . the letter! I could now so perfectly envision its drenched and dreadful contents. But the exquisite satisfaction of beholding it was never to be.

"Though I did not know then"—her voice rose distraughtly—"of the terrible crime Albrecht did after he used that young man."

Beth detached herself from her grandmother and stood up uncertainly. Her face was ravaged. The electrifying revelations of the past thirty minutes had produced a zombielike effect on the girl. But there had been no way to separate or soften the blows. They had come rapidly and relentlessly from the moment Karla had walked into Albrecht's room to find Beth transfixed with the evidence in her hands. The frightful train of explanations had been set in motion. Summoned from the lobby, I could only deplore and commiserate and console, and to Beth's inevitable cry, "But *why*?" the final words had to be spoken. What Barry had projected as a loving disclosure was now for Beth the shocking cause of her lover's crimes.

She'll survive, I thought, trying to feel callous. I reached for the phone and dialed my son's home in Brooklyn, again looking at my watch. Nine-fifteen. Pitch-black dark in the court outside the hotel. Albrecht would have picked up Sadd by now and be on his way back to Sixty-third Street. I shivered. Thank God Sadd had a key. Tina said hello.

"It's me, Clara. Can you handle three houseguests for one night?"

"Sure. Who?"

"Beth and her grandmother and me."

"Her *grandmother*? I thought—"

"Change of plan."

"You sound weird. Where are you?"

"Hotel Chelsea."

"What's up?"

"Tell you when I see you. Is it really okay to come?"

"Of course. We'll be a bit crowded but—"

"Crowded?"

"Sadd's here."

117

"Sadd!" It was a yelp. Beth and Karla standing at the window, murmuring in German, looked around.

"He came in a while ago with that friend of Beth's. The guy picked him up at the airport. Sadd said he was going to your place but we were nearer and he wouldn't have to bother you. Didn't I tell you he wouldn't last in Toronto with—"

"Tina, listen: You never got this phone call."

"I didn't? Okay."

"Where are you?"

"You mean in the house? Upstairs getting Hen to bed."

"Where's Henry?"

"Having a drink with Sadd and What's-his-name."

"Go down and send Sadd up to this phone—think of some excuse."

"Good. Hen's been begging Uncle Sadd to read him a story and Sadd's been dragging his feet."

"Typical. Tell him to haul ass—where *do* I learn such vulgarisms except from your husband?"

"Clara, is this serious?"

"Very, very."

"Henry will never forgive me if—"

"I'm okay. Get Sadd."

I turned and looked at my two companions, the old woman and the young one. I don't know which was more lost or helpless. Beth, of course, had the edge. She was blitzed. Now they were in a big chair, clinging together. I felt positively stalwart in the presence of such collapse, though my heart was in my mouth.

Sadd's voice said: "What now?"

"Sadd, the man you are sitting drinking with—"

"Was drinking with. He's gone."

"Gone!" Another yelp.

"He left as I came upstairs. What is the matter with you, Clara? I tried to be considerate and asked him to bring me here in order to spare you . . ."

I had dropped the receiver and was clawing about my knees for it. I got it back to my face long enough to say: "See you shortly, Tina will explain," and hung up. I stood up shaking.

118

"Beth, I hope to God you have your passport with you."

Dully: "Yes. And Albrecht's."

Albrecht's! It was too good to be true.

"I made him give it to me yesterday morning so we'd have them together at the airport tomorrow when I thought we were . . ." The mere thought did her in again.

I said briskly: "Give it to me—Albrecht's, I mean."

Weeping, she opened her pocketbook and took it out as if it was a snake.

I seized it and said: "I'm not sure that what I'm doing is wise or that it will work or that we'll be safe from Albrecht, but you both must realize we have to move fast."

Not quite so fast, however, that I didn't lean over and take a hand of each as they looked up at me pathetically.

"Listen, dears: Dollfuss was a tool, but Albrecht is a brain, and he's cold as ice. He followed Dollfuss from my house, or was waiting for him in the room, and after he threw him to his death he tore the first two pages out of that notebook so his name would be first and he'd get the call to come and do his identifying act."

Poor Karla was totally at sea, but Beth, despite her trauma, reacted to my words with jerky nods.

I plowed on: "We must expose him, we must. What he's done is too terrible. The thing is . . ." I dropped their hands and straightened up, looking over their heads at the dark window and thinking of another dark window. "The thing is to get out of here in ten minutes or we're goners." I took Adolf Ritter's passport from the bed and gave it to Beth, clamping her cold hand over it.

"Beth, go to Albrecht's room and put this someplace conspicuous, someplace he'll see it the minute he walks in there. Then get your stuff together—I hope you don't have much here. Thank God Karla hasn't unpacked. I said ten minutes but nine would be better. Meet me down at the desk in five."

I stuffed the envelope of cash into my pocketbook and pushed the sleepwalker out of the room.

At the front desk a bewildered but obliging clerk checked out the recently checked-in German lady and hoped nothing was wrong. No, I said, a personal emergency required her presence elsewhere for a few days. The clerk asked if Mr. Pohl, on whose charge the reservation was made, had been notified. I said I would leave him a note.

And now, might I ask a favor? "Do you have a manila envelope I can buy?"

No need to buy it, would this do? It would, and I slid Albrecht's passport inside. Did they have postage scales? They did. And now stamps, please.

"Those I insist on buying," I joked feebly, and slathered them on the envelope. I addressed it to myself, care of Colonel Barry Lockwood, Lake Winifred, Connecticut, summoned what moisture I could to my tongue, and sealed the envelope. I walked to the letter slot, which informed me that the next pickup was tomorrow morning at eight. That would be Tuesday. Reasonable to expect the thing would be in Lake Winifred on Thursday. I stood stock-still. The wedding day.

Beth and Karla came out of the elevator followed by luggage. At the desk I scribbled a note.

Albrecht,
    Remain here at the hotel. I will call you tomorrow night at nine o'clock. I think you'll like what I have to propose.

I signed my name, gave it to the clerk, and went with Karla and Beth into the street.

In the cab exhausted silence prevailed. The acquiescence of my two companions was complete, almost unnerving. Beth sat with her head thrown back against the seat, her eyes closed, her hand clutched in her grandmother's. Karla seemed more alert now. Presently she asked, not unjustifiably: "Where are we going?"

"To my son's home in Brooklyn, Karla. It's quite near. We'll spend the night there. Then, and I hate to sound arbitrary—"

Beth's head came up, her eyes automatically questioning. I took her notebook from her bag. "It means bossy, ordering people to do things," I said, writing. I closed the notebook

120

and looked out at the passing cables of the Brooklyn Bridge. I love the bridge at night and wanted to tell them to admire one of our glories, but to have them sightsee as we fled seemed antic.

I said, my eyes on the black water: "Then I want Beth to go back to Germany tomorrow as she planned. And I want you to go with her, Karla."

I looked at them, expecting to see them looking at each other in dismay, but both pairs of eyes were on my face. I went on:

"You'll be safe there. And if Beth wants to come back for her classes in a few weeks, well, by that time . . ." Go on, Clara, by that time what? Well, I told myself stoutly, by that time, in fact, by day after tomorrow, the WEDDING DAY (it had taken on upper case in my mind), if my plan works (granted, that's my bizarre and befuddled plan), then by that time Albrecht should be on ice. I ended lamely: "Well, by that time it should be okay." I added quickly: "Beth, do you have your plane ticket with you?"

She nodded: "I put it in my pocketbook this morning."

"Do you still have your room on Morningside Drive?"

"Yes. We couldn't find anything—" Oh, God, her face told me, was it only this morning they looked for another place together?

"Are there any valuables in your room?"

"No."

"Does your landlady know you plan to be away for a few weeks?"

"Yes."

"What airline are you on?"

"Lufthansa."

"Write down the flight number and the time."

I tore a page from the notebook and handed it to her, then turned my deployment skills on Karla.

"We can't be sure you'll get on Beth's flight, Karla, but we'll try for the nearest thing." I hesitated. "This will be expensive. A one-way ticket at a day's notice will be—" I was about to say "murder" but caught myself—"will be a lot of money. I'll be glad to help out, and we know that Barry would instantly—"

"No, please, you," said Karla quickly. "I will send the money back to you."

The mere mention of Barry's name seemed to dissolve both of them again. Beth began to sob and Karla gulped and choked and I looked desperately out of the cab window to note with relief that we were turning into Willow Street. I rapped on the window and told the driver the number. He began to slow.

I said briskly: "We're here. Let's try to shape up. It's been awful but all will be well"—keep up the brave chatter, Clara—"and my son and his wife will do everything they can to help."

"Henry and Tina, they are so nice, Umi." Beth mopped her eyes and ran her hands through her hair, which was in glorious, Gorgonlike disarray. Sadd won't sleep all night, I thought, squelching a smile, and there he was on the sidewalk, flashlight in hand, waving our driver to the curb.

My son's home was a plain old house at the top of some steep steps. He and Tina had slaved on it and made it charming, though they still retained their affectionate early name for it, Nice Ugly. Now they both appeared on the top step and Henry descended for the bags. Sadd paid the driver and I thanked him and said: "Sadd, this is Mrs. Spenhoff, Beth's grandmother."

Karla murmured: "Twice we have had taxis today and I have not paid."

"Mrs. Spenhoff"—Sadd took her hand—"for the pleasure of seeing your granddaughter I would pay for a taxi around the world. Let me have that case."

He took her small bag and her arm, and with Beth on the other side, they got Karla up the steps. I followed, calling back: "Henry, leave all the bags in the front hall. They go out again tomorrow."

In the living room we stood around aimlessly, no one making a move to sit down. I pulled the envelope of cash, wedged

122

in and bulging, from my pocketbook and said: "Tina, put this somewhere. It's twenty thousand dollars."

This only enriched the craziness of the situation, but my daughter-in-law, unfazed, walked to a secretary and laid the envelope in the bottom drawer. She locked it, dropped the key into a dish of paper clips, and said: "I have sandwiches."

We disposed of Karla and Beth at the earliest possible moment. Karla was in a state of near collapse and Beth's one concern was for her grandmother. Tina and I helped her get the poor lady upstairs where the pull-out double bed in Henry's study was made up and Tina said she hoped they'd be comfortable. "Clara, you're down in the dining room on the divan. Sadd goes in Hen's room in the bunk bed."

Sadd in a bunk bed after three nights in Toronto. He'd never forgive me. We went downstairs, leaving Beth to get Karla to bed.

No one had as yet said a word about our freaky arrival, but now I was in for it. We sat down and Sadd said: "Clara, this beats all."

"Begin at the beginning, Mom." Henry handed me a cognac. "And don't skip anything this time."

"Yes," I admitted, "I did some skipping last time I talked to you." I sipped my cognac gratefully.

"I have the impression," said Sadd, "that I have missed a great chunk of events."

"You all have."

Tina said: "Wait. Clara, you have no bag."

"No bag, no money, and I can't go home. Albrecht will be watching my place."

They looked startled. Henry said: "Albrecht? Beth's guy? He was just here. He seems harmless."

I looked at my watch. "He hasn't been harmless since about nine o'clock, when he got back to his room."

Sadd said: "Talk."

I did, disjointedly, backing up for Sadd's benefit, then plunging on to get to the events at the Chelsea. When I'd finished, they sat looking at me in rather stunned silence. I finished my cognac and put my head back on the sofa, feeling exhausted and drained.

Henry, who had still been on baggage detail when I gave Tina the money, said: "Where's the twenty grand?"

"In that drawer." Tina pointed. "Key's in the dish."

Henry got it out and counted it. He said: "I'll put this in the office safe tomorrow," and started to replace it. Then he said: "What's this?"

He loosened something stuck to the inside of the brown envelope. It was an ecru one, fattish, with several German stamps, wrinkled as if it had been wet, streaked with something red. Henry, his eyes on my face, pulled out sheets of dirty, crackling paper.

Tina got up and came and sat beside me. Sadd gave me a small, wry salute.

Henry said: "Shall I read it—or try to? It's pretty far gone and my German is lousy."

"Just the gist," I said swallowing, feeling no sense of vindication, only great sadness.

Between them Henry and Sadd pieced together fateful phrases regarding Albrecht's master plan, ending with the words—Sadd claimed these were an exact translation—"And what the hell is taking you so long?"

"No signature, just the letter A, so it couldn't be used as evidence," said Henry. "But there's a nice bit of poetic justice about the address." He held up the envelope. " 'Dollfuss Moltke' is almost completely obliterated by Anna's blood."

We were silent till Henry said: "Do you want to keep it, Mom?"

"No. No."

Henry put the envelope of money back in the drawer and locked it. Then he went to the fireplace and took a long match from a decorative box of them, struck it, and laid the ugly mass on the hearth.

Tina said, as we watched it burn: "I wonder why Albrecht even kept the awful thing. It had served its purpose."

The same thought having occurred to me, I said: "I'm not

sure he even knew it was in there. He must have been moving pretty fast—a quick check to be sure that was the money, then on to secure Adolf's passport."

"And why not destroy *that*?" demanded Sadd. "Of all the incriminating things to keep—"

"But valuable," said Henry. "Passports are worth a lot of money to certain people."

"That's what I figured," I said. "Albrecht was just biding his time till he could pick up some extra bucks." I shivered. "He must be beside himself for money."

With the hearth brush Henry swept black fragments into the fireplace. Then he came over and stood before me.

"Mom, I don't like this. It's bad enough to lose the dough and lose Beth, but Albrecht is going to be like a mad dog when he realizes you have his passport."

"I don't have it. I told you I mailed it to Barry's?"

"Yes, why in God's name did you do that?"

"I have a sort of plan. But first and foremost I want Beth and Karla safely out of the country."

"Which reminds me." Tina stood up. "I'm going up to see how they're doing."

She went out and Henry fixed me with a reflective eye. "A plan? Are you going to offer him a swap?"

"Something like that."

Sadd looked indignant. "But how would that bring the man to justice? He's a fiend! He should be . . ." Sadd boomed on and Henry walked up and down, his eyes on the floor.

He said: "The conditions would have to be foolproof. You'll need an ace."

"I think I know where I can get one."

"Promise me you won't try it alone."

"Try what alone?" Sadd interrupted one diatribe and launched into another, on the subject of the insanely risky escapades in which I involved my family.

"Well, one risk I *don't* intend to take," I said firmly, "and that's the risk of having anything spoil Doris and Barry's wedding."

Henry laughed and Sadd rolled his eyes. "A killer is among us and the woman is worried about a wedding!"

I said stubbornly: "I agree with Karla and I'm going to honor her wish: there's not going to be a cloud on Barry's happiness. He's been too great."

They were silent, then Sadd said, unexpectedly: "One has to admit he's done right by both his women."

"He certainly sacrificed a bundle for them," said Henry.

I thought of the pleasure it was going to be to return Barry's money to him. Tina came back to say that Karla was sound asleep and Beth too, still fully clothed, on the bed beside her.

"I guess the poor kid passed out before she could even get undressed. I just threw a blanket over her."

"Good idea." I stood up. "I'm about to pass out myself. Tina, do you have a nightgown I can borrow?"

I went off to my divan, trying not to envision Sadd's face when he was ushered to the bunk bed.

I slept as if I'd been poleaxed, and wakened to find Tina beside me with a cup of coffee and the announcement that Beth was gone and so was the twenty thousand dollars.

17

I SAT UP YANKING AT THE NIGHTGOWN INTO which about half of me fit.

I said: "Does Karla know?"

"Yes. She woke up to find Beth gone. She's distraught."

"Where is she?"

"In the kitchen with Sadd."

"Who realized the money was gone?"

"Henry. He had an early client so he left about the time of Hen's school bus."

I remembered groggily something about putting the cash in the office safe. I struggled up.

"Tina, you should go to work too. I've disrupted you enough."

"I can wait. I brought you Henry's robe."

"Thank you, dear." I put it on, then gulped some coffee and said: "What's your bet?"

She shrugged. "I don't know the girl well enough to bet. I suppose if she's mad about Albrecht she'll do anything for him."

I usually braid my hair at night, but last night I'd been too exhausted. The mirror over the divan showed me something resembling the Witch of Endor. I said, making a sloppy braid: "It's one reason I wanted Albrecht's passport out of my hands. I was in doubt about her."

But that much doubt? I tied Henry's robe about me, feeling disappointment take belated effect. I'd have put money on Beth. Well, you never know, I platitudinized to myself and wondered if Beth's defection would queer my plan. I went into the kitchen, a big, old-fashioned one with a lovely, venerable refectory table Tina had found. Karla slid out of the chair next to Sadd and came to me. In her pretty blue robe and slippers she looked like a withered child, and reached about to my chin as I put my arms around her.

Sadd was declaiming: "We've got to realize there are other possibilities. Beth has probably taken that money—she knows Barry originally expended it for her—and gone someplace to recover herself. She knows her grandmother is in good hands and she wants to be alone to sort things out."

Nobody had a comment on this upbeat scenario, and I led Karla back to the table and said: "Split a corn muffin with me. And I'd love some more coffee."

Tina poured it, saying: "Should Mrs. Spenhoff go back alone today?"

"Yes, today!" It was Karla, unexpectedly vehement. "I have caused worry enough for you all. I will go home where I belong."

Actually, I thought, a return to Sunny Acres, or whatever it was called, with its daily bridge game, must seem rather alluring at this point. I felt almost a twinge of envy as I spread marmalade and said: "I sure hope it can be today, Karla. Tina, will you get on the phone to Lufthansa and see what can be done? Beth wrote the number of her flight to Frankfurt. The paper is in my pocketbook, wherever that is."

Sadd said gently: "I don't mean to open the wound afresh, but won't any airline do now?"

Tina and I looked at each other. Karla's eyes were on her corn muffin, which she was eating a crumb at a time.

Tina said: "True, any one," and went into the dining room. For something to do I spread more marmalade. Now Tina was back with my pocketbook and I said: "Use my credit card."

She took the receiver from the kitchen wall and dragged it on its long cord into the pantry for easier listening; Sadd had started to talk in a loud voice as he stood up.

"I'm going upstairs to take a nap, and please do not remind me that it is only ten o'clock in the morning. I spent the night under a bouncing boy on a squeaky spring."

He looked at me balefully and I felt suddenly impatient. I said: "Oh, tough luck. I wish I had your troubles."

My voice must have betrayed my distress, confusion, and concern, for Sadd suddenly sat down again and Karla stood up.

"I must dress." She kissed me. "I will soon be gone."

She went off and we sat silent. Tina's voice, negotiating with some airline, came to us from the pantry.

Finally Sadd said: "Last night you and Henry were talking about some sort of 'plan' and I'm afraid I interrupted you. Would you care to discuss it now?"

"Yes, if you won't start to rant and rave and tell me it's insane."

"Okay."

Sadd never says "okay." He considers it "slang that has insidiously been legitimized" and always says "all right." His use of it now indicated to me that he was off guard and conciliatory. Perhaps worried. Me too.

I said: "The wedding is Thursday, but not till six P.M."

"Will you forget that blasted wedding?"

"But it's part of my plan."

"I thought you said nothing was going to interfere with the nuptials."

"It isn't! And see—you're already carping—" I broke off, visited by a ghastly thought. "Sadd! I have nothing to wear! I'm in a baggy wreck of a suit and I can't go home!"

Sadd exploded and Tina called: "Will you two shush?" She said something else into the phone, then came back to replace the receiver. She said, with an odd expression: "There's a cancellation on Beth's flight and Mrs. Spenhoff has it."

We looked at each other. Cancellation. Beth? Albrecht? Neither? Why not both? The heck with it—Karla was on.

Tina said: "One problem. You don't have a lot of time. Less than two hours. I wish I could take her, Clara, but I should get to the office."

129

I jumped. "Of course you should. Can we use your car? We'll drop you."

"Fine."

Sadd said darkly: "By 'we' I hope you mean you and Mrs. Spenhoff."

"By 'we' I mean anybody who is gentleman enough to help two poor old ladies handle that horror show at Kennedy."

"There goes my nap."

"Oh—and Tina—do you have a charge at A&S?"

Two-thirds of the tedious drive to Kennedy was made in silence. I'd placated Sadd somewhat by suggesting he take the wheel, a heroic gesture on my part, as his driving is erratic. Sadd boasts about his record, which, he says, after sixty years of driving, is "damn good." An imprecise claim and not reassuring as one sits beside him.

Karla, whom I'd tucked in the backseat under an afghan, was spared any apprehension. She was asleep ten minutes out.

Finally Sadd said dreamily: "If I were driving to the Sarasota airport now, the trip would be about twenty minutes and we'd just about now be passing the attractive campus of New College. The temperature would be a balmy seventy degrees and the palm—"

"Sadd," I said, "how is this poor old soul going to manage at the Frankfurt airport?" The question had bothered me since we left. "I'm tempted to cable the retirement home—tell them she's arriving."

"There are taxis. The lady herself said she hasn't footed one yet."

"But suppose it's an enormous distance. Think of the cost."

"Clara, there has already been enough money spent on this nutty nightmare to *buy* a taxi. What's a few dollars more? And the blithe way in which you use your credit card—"

"She'll send me the money. I trust Karla. I'm not worried."

130

But I was, and not about money. Karla would be alone in the plane, alone arriving, alone replying to the surprised inquiries about her sudden return, alone to speak or not speak about Albrecht, and above all, alone to worry about Beth. I glanced back at the tiny, sleeping form, the peaceful pale face—the last peaceful look it would wear for a while, I thought with compassion. Then I looked at my watch and gasped.

"What happened to the time?"

"It's running out. And the traffic's been bad, which is like saying the earth is round."

I didn't dare tell Sadd to hurry—that would be a true risk of life—but my agitated moans and mutterings made him nervous, so the result was almost the same. One particularly bad swerve brought Karla out of her nap, and she said wistfully, as children do: "How much farther?"

"Almost there, Karla," I said. "We're a little pressed for time so I think Mr. Saddlier will just let us off where we can put your bags through. You and I will go to the gate. It will probably be close to boarding time."

I was sweating a little. The thought of missing the plane and having to bring this aged waif back with us . . . And, oh God, the wedding on Thursday! The airport sign came into view and Sadd, probably having similar thoughts, went under it like a bullet.

"Everybody look for Lufthansa," I croaked, and Karla was the first to see it.

Edging into the three-deep line of cars at Departures, Sadd stopped and said: "Let's make a leap from here," a grotesque suggestion considering our mean age, but he was amazingly nimble and got the bags to the sidewalk as I got Karla to the bags. Then he went to the entrance and peered inside.

"Clara, I'll park and wait for you in that bar. Safe trip, Mrs. Spenhoff, and I enjoyed meeting—shut your bloody mouth, I'm coming!" The last in reply to a cab driver's yell.

I looked at my watch and breathed a bit easier. We were going to make it—barely, perhaps, but make it. Karla's bags were dispatched and we reached the crowded area at our gate, breathless but triumphant, with ten minutes till boarding time. We sank into seats and my game little companion gasped: "Do I have time for the lavatory?"

"Sure you do. I see it right over there. We have ten whole minutes."

Karla was only gone for five of those ten minutes, but it happened in less than three.

Beth's hair, always a beacon, caught my eye through the surging crowd. She was standing near the gate, straight, tense, watching. My joy was such that I didn't want to move at once, but just to bask in relief. I'd wait till Karla returned, then we'd go to the girl together. As I sat looking at her with renewed fondness, suddenly she moved forward, her arms outstretched. But not to me. Ten feet away Barry pushed through the crowd, reached her, and she was in his arms.

I'm almost certain they didn't speak. Then Beth moved, reached into her bag and took out the envelope of money. Barry shook his head, she pressed it against his chest, and he thrust it inside his coat. She put her hands on his shoulders and turned him around, touched her cheek to his back for an instant, then gave him a little push. He turned back, kissed her, and went.

At my side Karla was picking up her carry-on. "I heard them say 'boarding' in the lavatory."

Did you, Karla? Did you? I didn't hear a thing.

I moved with her toward the gate, and Beth was upon us.

In the bar Sadd said: "What did I tell you?"

"You told us"—I sipped my drink luxuriously—"that she'd gone off to brood somewhere and spend the money."

"I said there were other possibilities, and that was one of them."

"And thank God, this was another." I leaned back in the plastic armchair and brooded a bit myself. Tonight I must call Albrecht. A mad dog, Henry had said. But that analogy brought to mind fiery rage, and Albrecht's, I felt, would be icy cold. Deadly. Calculating. I had deliberately resisted en

132

visioning his initial reaction to the collapse of his life, but I was sure he had not ranted, and he would risk. I was his only chance.

Sadd was saying: "Did Beth have time to tell you why she decided to take off this morning?"

"No. She just said, 'Tina will tell you.'"

18

"SO, TINA, TELL US." I LOOKED AT THE CLOCK on the mantel. Twenty minutes to nine. I envisioned Albrecht sitting by the phone and I quaked a bit.

Hen put his head between the sliding door that divided the living room and the dining room and yelled: "Ready?"

"Five minutes, Hen," said his father. "Practice some more. Last time you didn't know your part."

We were seated in a line before the doors. Sadd had fortified himself with a drink and Tina held the prompter's script.

She said: "As I walked into my office the phone was ringing. It was Beth. She was very upset. She knew we must think she'd acted badly, but she woke up early with an overwhelming desire to see Barry, tell him she *knew*, and give him back the money herself. She took a cab to a car rental place and actually got on the road, sure she could make Lake Winifred and back by plane time."

"Innocents abroad," murmured Sadd.

"You can believe she didn't get far before she realized it was mission impossible. She stopped at a gas station in the Bronx and called Barry. No answer. She called Doris and poured out her heart. Doris said Barry was in New York doing last-minute business with his insurance agent. He would probably call her before he left Manhattan, and if he did, she'd tell him Beth's plane time."

"That woman should get a medal," said Henry.

Hen yelled again: "Ready?"

"Ready!" we chorused.

The sliding doors were dragged open by a pair of grimy

134

hands. I think there were two other children besides Hen, and I'm almost sure the play was about robots, for there was a great deal of aluminum foil in evidence; but my mind was on Albrecht. Had he stayed put? Would he answer? Would he buy? At one point I whispered to Henry: "Did you get that information for me?"

He whispered back: "Yes. You can get a warrant issued."

"Even if the crime has been committed in another state?"

"If you have foolproof evidence, which you do."

"Will you go with me?"

"Sure will."

". . . before we depart this galaxy forever," prompted Tina. It sounded encouragingly like a curtain line, and sure enough, the doors slid across. We applauded mightily, the actors came out for bows, I hugged Hen and made my escape toward the stairs. Henry and Tina called "Good luck" and Sadd handed me a brandy.

I sat at the desk in Henry's study and stared at the phone. I'd never been a particularly good actress; in plays at school I'd been self-conscious and unconvincing. But, I told myself, this wasn't acting, this was *selling*. I must sell Albrecht on myself as a woman of unexpectedly venal qualities. My husband once said that venality is hard to fake when you're dealing with an honest soul. Only a person as unprincipled as you are attempting to seem will accept and believe. You are talking his language.

I took a sip of brandy and rang the Chelsea. I asked for Albrecht Pohl and he answered.

"Albrecht, this is Clara Gamadge and here is my proposal: I will sell you back your passport for ten thousand dollars."

I expected a pause, at least a short, memorial pause for the burial of my Nice Lady image. Instead he said immediately: "Where would I get such an amount of money? You took the twenty."

"Yes, the twenty *helps*. But actually"—a faint note of apology—"it only makes me realize I could use a bit more."

"You don't appear to be in need of money, Mrs. Gamadge."

"Neither did you, Albrecht."

POW! Got you there, I hope. You and me both, Mister. Calm on the outside, desperate on the inside. I went on confidentially: "It's a nightmare, isn't it, being in this kind of trouble? Appearances don't change much at first, but one knows it's only a matter of time. I don't know about you, but I'm perfectly willing to admit I brought it on myself. My husband left me very well off and for a while I managed things quite nicely, but speculation has always been my weak point. Oh, I don't mean I'm *destitute*"—a little laugh to indicate my predicament was of the Beautiful People Only variety—"it's just that, well, my son warned me. He's so like his father, very conservative—almost straitlaced. I've been dreading telling him, maybe even having to borrow from him, and a few dollars now would—oh, need I go on?" I hoped not; I was running out. Time now to clinch my depravity.

"And in case you think I might have been shocked by the fate of Adolf Ritter, I *wasn't*. He was one of those awful Nazis and deserved what he got. Besides, Albrecht, to be quite honest, you did the brainwork." Was there such a word as "brainwork"? Before I could decide, Albrecht said: "I repeat: Where would I get ten thousand dollars?"

I made my voice worried. "Oh, dear . . ."

Suddenly: "Where is Elisabeth?"

"Over mid-Atlantic by now, with her grandmother. It seemed the best thing. This has been very trying for both of them, especially since Beth now realizes what brought it all about. To be quite honest, Albrecht"—hadn't I just used that expression?—"I'm bored with the whole thing, and I imagine you are too. Whatever was to be made has been made, but I do have this teeny, unexpected advantage and I'd like to make use of it if possible. I just had a thought: I'll give you your passport if you'll give me Adolf Ritter's."

I expected the Pause of Pauses, but again he said at once: "What do you want with his?"

"I understand from my son that passports are worth quite a bit in certain markets."

"Does he have connections in these markets?"

"Heavens, I wouldn't *tell* him!" Shock and horror. "I only asked him in the most academic way. I told you how straitlaced he is." I hurried on desperately. "You and I are rather alike, Albrecht—practical, I suppose you'd call it— and I truly would like to see you get out of the country. You've had rather a raw deal in all this."

Sympathy was vitally important at this point and I was laying it on with a shovel lest Albrecht perceive the fatal flaw in my proposal and say: Why don't you simply sell *my* passport? The prospect of flight must be dangled so close that he could not see around it.

Now he made a sound something like a groan. "What do you propose?"

Oh, thank God. Careful now, Clara. Make it sound safe and simple. I drew a breath.

"Colonel Lockwood is getting married on Thursday in Lake Winifred, Connecticut, a little town about three hours from New York. The wedding is at six and my family and I will be going up. If you will meet me at the Colonel's house at five, we'll make the swap."

His voice was harsh. "Why all that distance? Why can't we meet here? If you have fear of me we can meet in a public place."

"I don't have your passport, Albrecht. I mailed it to Colonel Lockwood's house. To be quite honest"—that was getting to be my favorite phrase—"I didn't trust Beth not to return it to you."

I interpreted this pause as bitter. The question that came next was unexpected.

"Where are you now, Mrs. Gamadge?"

"With friends."

"I went to your place last night"—I'll bet you did!—"and then I guessed you were with your son in Brooklyn."

I felt a chill. I'd quite forgotten he'd been here. The last thing I wanted was Albrecht showing up. I said: "Albrecht,

137

wherever I am, your passport is in Lake Winifred. If you want it, come there."

"It is very elaborate." His voice was grim. "And Colonel Lockwood—"

"Colonel Lockwood doesn't know you exist." I was so happy to speak the truth at last, it must have rung in my voice. I went on cheerfully: "The envelope with your passport is addressed to me for holding. Come to the Colonel's at five o'clock and bring Ritter's. The exchange will be very civilized, Albrecht. You might even get a piece of wedding cake."

He said slowly: "Mrs. Gamadge, you may or may not be—there is an expression, I believe—'on level'—but if I am to take this chance let me remind you of something: my possession of Ritter's passport can in no way connect me with the dead man on Morningside Drive. I could have found it on the street or in a trash bin."

"Of course, but why—"

"That dead man was nameless, un-identi-fi-able." He pronounced it laboriously but correctly. "Keep saying that to yourself. Should you have any ideas which—"

"Albrecht, we're wasting time. I hope you still have your rental car. Here are the directions to Lake Winifred."

The next morning, in the kind of torrential downpour that windshield wipers can hardly handle, Henry and I zigzagged our way to First Avenue and made fairly good time up to One hundred twenty-sixth Street. We walked into the somber structure of the headquarters to be greeted by Dick Swiveller, who gave me a surprised, pimply smile.

"Mrs. Gabbage, isn't it?"

"That's right. I'm so glad you're here, Officer. This is my son, Henry. He's a lawyer. We've come about that dead man with no identification—the one with the German name who was found on Morningside Drive."

"Yeah?"

"We know his real name—not the one he used—and the person who killed him."

Dick looked from me to Henry. "I'll get the boss."

He led us to an office with a desk and a file and disappeared.

I said: "Who is the 'boss'?"

"The precinct captain."

I sat down shakily. "Your father always did this end of things. Will you take over, dear?"

Henry nodded and roamed around the room. Presently a gaunt, sallow man, perfectly in keeping with his surroundings, came in and said he was Captain Redmond. He went to the file, took out a folder, and as he laid it on the desk the little spiral notebook slid out. I kept my eyes on it as Henry started to talk.

"On Monday, May eighth, at about five P.M., a young man named Adolf Ritter was involved in a traffic accident on East Sixty-third Street between Fifth and Madison. What precinct would that be?"

Dick Swiveller, who had come back and was leaning in the door, said: "Nineteen."

"The accident was the result of a skid, no fault of Ritter's. The rain was heavy and he killed a woman, a friend, in fact, whom he'd come to pick up. There was a full report, no charges made. Ritter was German, a tourist here, his German driver's license was in order and so was his passport. I assume all this would be on file down at that precinct?"

The captain nodded.

"Five days later, last Saturday, Ritter was found dead in the court of a student rooming house on Morningside Drive where he lived and where he had not given his real name. He called himself Dollfuss Moltke. He'd been robbed of everything, including his passport, and the only thing left on him was that notebook on your desk with some names and addresses. The first name was that of an acquaintance, Albrecht Pohl, also German and a tourist, who was staying at the Hotel Chelsea and who, with my mother—this lady—and a young woman, Elisabeth Bauer, a friend of the dead man's, came to identify him—but, of course, as Dollfuss Moltke, the name he used."

Bravo, Henry. I couldn't have done nearly so well. I'd have rambled and stumbled and backed and filled. Captain Redmond, who had not taken his eyes from the file, said: "Go on."

"We now have proof that Pohl went to Ritter's room the night before, robbed him, killed him, and took his passport. Pohl believed that he had rendered the body nameless and unidentifiable, but he either forgot or did not know about the accident on Sixty-third Street, which produced a full file on the dead man, including, I assume, fingerprints."

"You say you have proof." The captain looked up. "What proof?"

"Ritter's passport was found concealed in Pohl's room together with a large sum of money paid to him by a friend of ours whom they were blackmailing."

The captain looked at Dick Swiveller and said: "Get on the phone to Nineteen." Dick departed eagerly. The captain closed the file. "Who found the passport and the money?"

I cleared my throat. "I did. I purposely went looking for them because I had reason to believe he was guilty. I returned the money to our friend but left Adolf Ritter's passport."

"Does Pohl know it was you who entered his room?"

"Yes. I talked to him on the phone last night."

"Where is he?"

"Still at the Chelsea."

The gaunt face looked a little bewildered. "Why is he hanging around if he knows the game's up? Why hasn't he left the country?"

I looked at Henry, who was looking at the ceiling. I said: "He can't leave, Captain. I have his passport."

The captain's eyes took on a slight glaze. "How did you get it?"

"I stole it."

"What my mother means is—"

"What I mean is, Captain, I took it in order to offer him a swap."

"What *I* mean is, ma'am, how did you get it, or have it or steal it or whatever you did?"

140

"His young lady friend gave it to me. Elisabeth Bauer. She—She realized what he'd done."

"Where is she?"

"She has returned to Germany." I was getting impatient; I had a rendezvous. "I probably acted rather officiously, Captain, but it all happened quite fast. She was with me when I found the evidence, and I was afraid I had put us both in jeopardy. My idea was to make an exchange. Pohl's own passport back for Ritter's. I told him I needed money and planned to sell Ritter's on the black market—or Pohl's, it made no difference—but I was willing to help him leave the country because I felt sorry for him."

Henry looked at me with pride, the captain with horror.

I hurried on: "Of course, my intention is that Albrecht Pohl be arrested with the dead man's passport still in his possession. May I tell you how it can be done tomorrow afternoon?"

Rather dazedly, the captain said: "The identification has to check out first."

"Of course. And when that nice young officer comes back and says it does, here's what I suggest."

But before I could suggest, Dick Swiveller was back.

"It checks out, Chief."

19

I SAID AS WE CAME OUT: "TWO VISITS HERE IN the same week, not to mention a trip to the morgue. Dad would laugh."

"Laugh and love it." Henry put his arm around me as we walked to the car.

I said: "Is it going to work, Henry?"

He didn't reply at once, and my heart sank. We drove three or four blocks before he said: "Don't be disappointed if A, they can't get a warrant this fast, B, the police in Lake Winifred don't follow through, or C, Albrecht doesn't show up."

" 'C' is the only one I'm sure of. But if the police don't come, what do I do?"

"You give Albrecht his goddam passport back and let him split. Enough is enough, Mom. Nobody engaged you, nobody assigned you, nobody's hot to have Albrecht arrested but you. Barry's got his money back, Beth's eyes are opened, end of movie."

Oh, but poor Anna. I said: "I just hate to see . . ."

"Justice not done, and all that? You lived with Dad long enough to know how often it isn't. Coffee?"

"Yes."

Henry turned into a Burger King and went in. I sat still, depressed, and in sudden fear. When he came out with the coffee I said: "Henry, suppose Albrecht's passport doesn't get delivered at Barry's tomorrow."

"When was it picked up?"

"Early yesterday."

142

"It'll get there. Maybe today, certainly tomorrow. Quit worrying."

Panic-stricken, I envisioned the mail truck pulling into Barry's drive and Albrecht seizing the delivery. He would escape with both prizes owing to my imbecile inefficiency. How had I conceived of a plan so fraught with possibilities of disaster?

Henry looked at me and said: "Stop brooding. Think of the wedding and how happy you are for Barry. He's had his justice."

But had Anna? My friend.

We were on the bridge and the clock on the dash read one-thirty. I said: "Drop me at A&S and go to your office."

The cheerful din of the department store had a perversely depressing effect on me. I wandered through Misses Dresses thinking of Anna and how she loved to shop and would drag me, hating it, with her. Always slim, she'd remained a nifty size 11 till the day she . . . died. Often, she would stroll off while I was enduring the trauma of the dressing room and return with a pretty piece of jewelry or a scarf that she'd present to me with such words as "this says thanks for being such a good sport and I'll buy you lunch."

"Are you all right, ma'am?"

I nodded and with one hand scrounged in my pocket for a tissue; with the other I pulled something off a rack. "Do you have this in a size 14?"

"If not"—tactful smile—"maybe 12?"

"If not"—grim smile—"maybe 16?"

And so the afternoon took its merry course and I finally emerged onto the street with two boxes, an enormous one containing a pale green, raw silk suit, and a shoe box with "bone" pumps—"We don't say 'tan,' madam, we say 'bone' "—to find that the rain had turned into a heavy mist and all Brooklyn looked like Baker Street. I started hailing cabs and finally got one.

It was only three o'clock but no ray penetrated to the shrouded street. Traffic crept. Did my driver know Willow Street, not far from there—near the bridge? He did. I lay back, closed my eyes, and thought about the bone shoes. The heels were higher than I liked. Why had I let that salesman talk me into them? I'd probably wear them tomorrow and never again . . . I suppose I dozed.

"Three fifty, lady."

I sat forward dazedly and looked at the meter. There appeared to be a small black figure standing on it. I took out my wallet and when I looked back the odd illusion had vanished. The figure was that of a man in a dark coat standing at the end of the street.

Albrecht, or I hadn't bought bone shoes.

The mist still hovered but wasn't as dense here. The figure didn't move. I looked up at the front of Nice Ugly, then at my watch. Three forty-five. Hen would be home from school, which meant Teresita was there too. Why should she prevent him from running out if he should glimpse Gran from a window? I quickly pulled a five-dollar bill from my wallet and flourished it.

"Will you do me a big favor and help me up the stairs? These boxes are so heavy and awkward."

Fortunately the driver was young and big. He hotfooted it around to my door, seized my purchases, and made for the steps.

"Wait!" Didn't the idiot know he was a bodyguard, not a porter? I clambered out and reached him in six steps, tucking my arm through his on the side away from Albrecht. I was whisked up the stairs and, over my shoulder, saw Albrecht move a step, then stop.

"Thank you so much." I fumbled in my pocketbook for the bill, which I'd thrust back should there be a delay in answering the door. But Teresita's smiling face appeared, the five vanished into a grubby fist, and I was inside.

How long had Albrecht's vigil been? How long would it last? I said nothing to the family about it that evening as we discussed what Henry called "The Albrecht Trap," nor did any of them say they'd seen him, nor did I look out of the window once.

* * *

The next day was glorious, a "someday-in-May-wedding-day" à la the Andrews Sisters. Henry and Tina returned from the office at noon. They went upstairs to change as I made salads. Sadd was on the phone arranging for a return to paradise next day.

"Can somebody take me to La Guardia tomorrow at two? Maybe somebody whom I heroically helped by piling out to Kennedy when—"

"Okay, okay, I'll take you." I went to don my new finery and we sat down to lunch, not a bite of which, I suddenly realized, could I eat.

"You all look very elegant." Sadd gazed around the table. "I didn't come prepared to attend a wedding. Thank you for washing my one shirt, Tina. But I still don't see"—he buttered a roll—"how this is to be accomplished without a degree of sensationalism. A police car in Barry's driveway with his wedding in progress?"

I said: "You can't see his driveway from the church, and it's a whole hour before." But my dread on this very point had been mounting.

Tina said: "Have you alerted him?"

"No. I didn't want to till the last minute. When I get there I'll tell him."

"Decent of you," said Sadd.

Henry said: "When we get to Lake Winifred, why don't we stop at the police and see if—"

"I'm afraid to," I said. "Albrecht might be cruising around to see if we do."

"Would the place be that conspicuous?" Tina cut cake. "I can't believe 'the police' in Lake Winifred is more than one room and one policeman."

"I'd rather not stop. Great cake, Tina." I managed to swallow a morsel.

Sadd said: "I keep trying to think of that suave character who picked me up at the airport as a killer. I must say I felt no sinister vibrations, but then I'm the least psychic person on earth. My one reaction was to his great size."

"Yes," said Tina, "he certainly has the build for heaving

somebody out the window. No wonder Karla was scared of him. He could put her in his pocket."

All this was doing nothing for my appetite.

Henry said: "I wonder if he has a weapon."

Oh, God—a shootout as the organist strikes up. I put down my coffee cup and said: "Let's go now."

Henry looked at the clock. "We'll be a tad early."

"So might Albrecht."

Despite the lovely, dappled green that bordered the Taconic Parkway and the golden sunlight that poured down upon it, my spirits sank as we approached our destination. My nerves tightened unyieldingly, and the weird comparison occurred to me of the tiny rubber bands on the braces I used to wear on my teeth.

As we turned off the Taconic onto Route 44 Tina said: "Does anybody besides me have déjà vu?"

Henry nodded. "One week ago, the four of us, Anna's service."

Sadd said, with elaborate wistfulness: "And I first set eyes on the lovely Beth."

"And we all thought she was going to marry Barry." Henry chuckled. "Mom, do you know what color Albrecht's car is?"

"Oh, God—why? Where?"

"For Pete's sake, nowhere. Will you relax? I just thought I might drop you all off at Doris's and do a little touring to see if he's around town. Even if he saw me, so what? You told him we were all coming to the wedding, and I'm the sainted son who knows nothing about your sordid transaction. What do you say?"

I clasped and unclasped my pocketbook, then told myself to stop it. "I hate to descend on Doris too early."

"I just had a ghastly thought!" Tina sat up. "When do they leave for Greece?"

"Tomorrow," I said, "but they're going to New York tonight and I know what you're going to say." The same ghastly

146

thought had occurred to me. "Suppose their mail is being held for them at the post office."

"That would be as of tomorrow." Tina patted my hand. "All is well. Doris would want today's."

"Why?" I desperately hoped the reason would be valid.

Tina looked at me in surprise. "She's getting married. She'd want last-minute letters and presents."

The reason was wonderfully, beautifully valid.

Henry said: "But here's Son of Ghastly Thought: Does Barry have one of those rural postboxes at the end of the drive? Can Albrecht open it and help himself?"

"No, he cannot," I said. "I'll give myself credit for that one small precaution. Barry has a mail slot on his front door. It's a brass one I gave Barry and Anna as a house-warming present and Anna scratched their initials on the inside."

Sadd said: "I have the distinct impression of being in the middle of a Pink Panther movie."

"Oh, I wish it was funny," I moaned.

Tina said firmly: "Nothing more on the subject till we get there. Tell us who else is coming to the wedding."

"Besides Albrecht," murmured Henry with a grin. Then: "Sorry. Dumb joke."

"It's all right." I now felt what I believe is classically called "the calmness of despair." "Laugh your heads off at foolish Inspector Clara Clouseau."

"Tina asked you a question," said Henry.

"What? Oh—about the wedding? I really don't know. Barry's family is all gone. He had one sister who died young. Doris has a daughter who's going to stand up with her, and she said her son and his family are coming from Vermont. Sara and Eve, or course, and I guess friends and neighbors—"

"Mr. and Mrs. Hazen were invited," said Sadd. "I do hope they can make it and she doesn't forget her pictures."

"Where's the reception?" asked Tina.

"In the chapel hall."

Was this civilized, standard conversation taking place as I neared my appointment with a murderer? Henry's thoughts

147

must have been along the same line because he said: "I wasn't kidding when I wondered if Albrecht had a weapon. I don't want you out of my sight, Mom."

"That's impossible. I told Albrecht—"

"I don't care what you told him."

"Henry, please. Barry will be there. Why would Albrecht want to compound his crimes? I plan to take his passport out of the envelope so he can see it's the real McCoy—"

"Here we are," said Tina.

We turned at the lake, passed a caterer's van, and drew alongside the chapel. I sent one wild glance into the clearing across the road, and a ghostly, big old red Buick took filmy shape there. I felt a surge of rage that completely dispelled my depression.

Dammit, call me Lafayette. Anna, I am here!

I said: "Please stop, Henry. I'm getting out."

Henry always said that when he was a little boy he recognized a certain tone that said *this is your mother speaking*. Now he gave me a rueful smile, pulled into the chapel driveway, and stopped. None of them spoke as I got out, straightened the jacket of my new suit, and started down toward the granite marker on the corner of Barry's road.

I walked rather slowly on my too-high heels and, as I turned the corner, slower still, and not because of the heels. My throat felt as if a hand held it, and I was uncomfortably warm despite the perfection of the weather. I looked at my watch. Twenty minutes before five. I'd walk into Barry's house, tell him not to get out of the shower or stop shaving or interrupt whatever he was doing, ask if there was a piece of mail for me and where was it. Then I would come back out and wait for Albrecht.

Now I was passing Doris's house. The driveway was full of cars; family members would be gathered happily inside. Another few seconds and Barry's drive would be visible. Here it was.

A single car stood there. It wasn't Barry's. It was unmistakably Albrecht's. And Albrecht himself was unmistakably a madman.

148

His enormous form was coatless and he loomed on the top step before Barry's front door, bent grotesquely in the act of rolling a heavy stone planter off the step into a flower bed. It landed with a crash and he leaped after it and began to pull out handfuls of geraniums. All around was minor chaos. The doormat had been flung to the grass, flagstones were overturned, and ceramic lawn ornaments were in smithereens.

I walked up the front path, stopped ten yards from him and said: "Albrecht."

He straightened with an almost spastic jerk and turned and looked at me, muddy hands hanging at his side. He made no move, simply stood panting, looking at me with vacant eyes. I walked past him and up the three steps to the front door and took down a note taped to it. It read:

Doris,
    Back in twenty minutes, key in usual place.

And at that moment a police car turned into the drive, followed by Barry's car, followed by Henry's. I thought absurdly, Only Broderick Crawford is missing!, as the sound of car doors slamming shattered the air.

From the police car emerged a sherifflike figure and—Dick Swiveller!

"Hi, Mrs. Gabbage. Sure, I remember this guy."

Barry was hurrying toward me carrying something in a plastic cleaner's bag. I ran to him on the wobbly heels.

"Barry, I'm so sorry—"

"Are you okay? Who is this guy?"

"Did a piece of mail come for me today?"

"Yes, I put it—"

"Go in and get it and give it to that young officer." I looked around at Dick Swiveller, who was lifting Albrecht's coat from the grass. He took a flat green object from the breast pocket as Albrecht watched, still without moving. I turned back to Barry feeling a little dizzy. "Then *get changed*, Barry. You're being married in an hour!"

"But what—"

"Henry will explain."

Tina was beside me and I grabbed her hand and we hurried across the lawn toward the chapel, where festive figures were beginning to gather and Sara and Eve were waving to us.

As a radiant Doris and Barry exchanged vows, Henry, sitting beside me in the pew, whispered:

"I keep thinking about that note on Barry's front door."

"Me too," I whispered back.

"Where the heck do you suppose he hides the key?"

"I'd give anything to know."

"Was he in the Secret Service or something? His 'usual place' must be a beaut."

On my other side Sara whispered: "I hope Beth's granny can't make it for bridge next week. She gives me an inferiority complex," and I whispered back that no, I didn't think she could make it.

The clergyman, the same who had reminded us of our mortality at Anna's service, was now reminding us, at somewhat unnecessary length, that married life could indeed be a joy to those who were happy in the Lord. I trembled as Sadd leaned forward from the pew behind me and whispered that he would give the reverend gentleman exactly thirty seconds more. Tina, in the pew ahead, turned around and whispered to tell Sadd to shush, she could hear him from there. Eve, on the other side of Sara, leaned across and whispered that this was an especially lovely homily on marriage, wasn't it?

Mercifully, the loveliness ended and the organ pealed.

One more whisper came to me a few hours later in the chapel hall when the merrymaking was at its height: "Barry and I are going to sneak away. Walk over to his house with us."

Music and voices faded pleasantly behind us as we walked across the lawn. The night air was heavenly and the moon very bright. As we approached Barry's front door I was grateful to see that the scattered damage had been repaired, and only the empty planter, back on the top step, gave evidence of Albrecht's frenzied search.

Doris said: "What was all that commotion out here this afternoon?"

"I'll tell you in Greece," said Barry. He took out his key. "I'd love to carry you across the threshold, Mrs. Lockwood, but I'm afraid I'd get a hernia and Greece would be out."

Doris laughed joyously and I kissed them both.

"Bon voyage. But tell me something, Barry: where is the 'usual place' you hide your key?"

He chuckled. "That was an old trick of Anna's. She was forever losing her keys and finally she decided, when she went out during the day, if she just left a note saying the key was hidden someplace, anybody would assume the door was locked. But it never was."

They went in. I stood for a moment looking at the pale face of the door, so vulnerable, yet so impregnable. The two, high, bull's-eye glass windows stared down at me blankly as they must have stared down at Albrecht, destroying his own sanity.

I walked back across the silvery grass toward the party.

Thank you, Anna.

About the Author

Eleanor Boylan is the author of *Working Murder,* the first Clara Gamadge mystery, and as well as stories published in such magazines as *Ellery Queen* and *Alfred Hitchcock Mystery Magazine.* Born in New York, she raised her family in Boston and currently lives on Anna Maria Island in Florida. She is the niece of Elizabeth Daly, author of the Henry Gamadge mysteries and Agatha Christie's favorite writer.